GW00733127

MIDAS

I start the car and open the door. She looks a real mess. Her hair is tangled, her make-up smeared, her dress ripped right down to the waist. The first shot rings out. I watch as the woman falls forward and staggers. Suddenly blood appears on her shoulder and forearm. I put the car into gear as another shot rings out, and then a third. The shot sends her skidding the last two or three steps to my car, and the door slams shut. Her face bangs against the side window. I put my foot on the gas. Her face disappears with a jerk backwards and leaves a mess on the glass.

'And that woman who was shot to death was Nancy Tanner?'

'I swear, Mr Kirk. It was her face, her figure, her voice! But the crazy thing is, Mr Kirk — I saw her again today.'

About the Author

Wolfgang Jeschke was born in Czechoslovakia in 1936 and grew up in Stuttgart. He trained as a toolmaker and then studied literature and philosophy at Munich University. During the 1950s and '60s he wrote science fiction short stories and novellas; and then devoted himself chiefly to editing science fiction works. He is now responsible for the science fiction programme at Heyne publishers in Munich. His most recent novel before MIDAS was THE LAST DAY OF CREATION, published in 1981.

Wolfgang Jeschke

MIDAS

NEW ENGLISH LIBRARY
Hodder and Stoughton

Copyright © 1987
by Wolfgang Jeschke

First published in Germany
by Willhelm Heyne Verlag
in 1987

First published in Great
Britain in 1990 by New
English Library paperbacks

A New English Library
paperback original

*The characters and situations in
this book are entirely imaginary
and bear no relation to any real
person or actual happening.*

This book is sold subject to the
condition that it shall not, by way of
trade or otherwise, be lent,
re-sold, hired out or otherwise
circulated without the publisher's
prior consent in any form of
binding or cover other than that in
which it is published and without a
similar condition including this
condition being imposed on the
subsequent purchaser.

No part of this publication may be
reproduced or transmitted in any
form or by any means,
electronically or mechanically,
including photocopying, recording
or any information storage or
retrieval system without either the
prior permission in writing from
the publisher or a licence,
permitting restricted copying. In
the United Kingdom such licences
are issued by the Copyright
Licensing Agency, 33-34 Alfred
Place, London WC1E 7DP.

Printed and bound in Great Britain
for Hodder and Stoughton
Paperbacks, a division of Hodder
and Stoughton Ltd., Mill Road,
Dunton Green, Sevenoaks, Kent,
TN13 2YA. (Editorial Office:
47 Bedford Square, London
WC1B 3DP) by Cox & Wyman
Photoset by Chippendale Type,
Otley, West Yorkshire.

British Library C.I.P.

Jeschke, Wolfgang
    Midas.
    I. Title
833'.914[F]

    ISBN 0–450–50937–0

Contents

Once upon a time there was a cantankerous old tailor who drove his three sons away from home because he chose to believe the lies of a wicked goat rather than his sons' assurances to the contrary. The youths – somewhat naive, but very industrious – set off into the world to make their fortune. The eldest son became a carpenter and, as a going-away present from his master, received a magic table that spread itself with delicious food. The second apprenticed himself to a miller and was given a donkey that spewed forth shining gold pieces. The third became a lathe worker and his master made him a present of a sack with a magic club in it, which, on command, whipped out and beat anyone who deserved to be attacked. A thievish innkeeper exchanged the presents of the first two sons for a table and donkey without any magic qualities, and the sons made fools of themselves in the eyes of their relatives who had gathered to marvel at their fortune. But, with his magic club, the third son recovered the real table and donkey from the innkeeper and brought them home to everyone's delight.

'Is that all, Alice?'

'That's all.'

1

The Lives and Sorrows of Nancy Tanner

'I'm sure you've heard of Nancy Tanner,' the taxi driver said. He drove into a quiet side street and parked at the back entrance to a restaurant in Wolfendahl Street.

'The actress?'

'Yes.'

'I've seen some of her films on video,' I said. 'Why do you ask?'

He hesitated.

'Come on, out with it?'

He pulled a crushed packet of Benson and Hedges out of his shirt pocket, lit a cigarette, his fingers trembling, and blew the smoke against the windshield. 'I'm scared.'

'Why's that?'

'I can trust you, can't I, Mr Kirk?'

I shrugged my shoulders. 'You should know me well enough by now.'

'I actually saw her being murdered.'

'Nancy Tanner? Come off it! Where did you get such a crazy story? It would have been in all the papers! *What* exactly did you see?'

'It happened last week, the night of the 18th. I was waiting in my taxi down in the Korteboam Street at the back entrance to the officers' club – the door the officers use when they leave with the prostitutes who go there.

In order to impress their so-called lady friends, they usually give us a good tip. So, there I was, waiting in this filthy alley with rats running around and overflowing rubbish bins. Suddenly, without warning, the door bangs open and I hear loud music. Two figures stagger out, wrestling with one another, an officer and a tall, blonde lady. It's hard to see in the dreary neon light, but he's on the point of trying to make it with her there in all that filth. His pants are open and he grabs her dress and tears it open. He must have been really drunk. He pulls her towards him again and again and fumbles clumsily trying to get under her skirt. He doesn't succeed, though, because the woman is really very strong. He beats her in a mad rage, but she breaks loose and runs away screaming. He lands among the rubbish bins with such a thud that the rats scatter off in all directions. He picks himself up quickly and – I can't believe my eyes – pulls out a gun.

"Help me – help!" she screams, running towards my taxi. "Take me away from here! These beasts!" I start the car and open the door. She looks a real mess. Her hair is tangled, her make-up smeared, her dress ripped right down to the waist. The first shot rings out. I watch as the woman falls forward and staggers. She twists her outstretched hands like claws and crosses her arms protectively to cover her naked breasts. Suddenly blood appears on her shoulder and forearm. I put the car into gear as another shot rings out, and then a third. The shot sends her skidding the last two or three steps to my car, and the door slams shut. Her face bangs against the side window. Her eyes are already glassy and her mouth is wide open – I will never forget the sight. I put my foot on the gas. Her face disappears with a jerk backwards and leaves a mess on the glass. Two more shots shatter the rear window so I can't see. I drive as fast as I can to get out of the city, expecting at any moment to see an army police car following me.'

'And that woman who was shot to death was Nancy Tanner?'

'I swear, Mr Kirk. It was her face, her figure, her voice!'

'You said yourself you could hardly see anything, the lighting was so bad.'

'At the beginning, yes, but in the end, her face was no more than an arm's length away. But the crazy thing is, Mr Kirk – I saw her again today.'

'The same woman?'

'Nancy Tanner. I was driving up and down the Janadhipathi Mawatha looking for customers and suddenly, in broad daylight, I saw her again. She was walking arm in arm with a general, as beautiful as ever. Alive and kicking, as the saying goes. She was carrying a parasol in her hand and seemed in a good mood. In fact, she looked a little tipsy. I was so flabbergasted I slammed on the brakes and someone almost banged into me from behind. Several cars hooted me and the general looked my way. A shiver went through my spine. I was glad that they had not flagged me down and I tried to disappear behind my sunglasses. At that moment, she also glanced at me and there was no doubt left in my mind at all – it was Nancy Tanner alright.'

'Why are you so sure?'

'Because I loved her. You must have seen her film *The Tea Plucker*, filmed in Sri Lanka during the Tamil wars?'

I could well remember the trashy monumental epic – a story about love for one's fellow men, international understanding and passion. It had won four or five Oscars. She played the role of an American journalist who succeeded in bringing a young wounded Tamil terrorist safely through the enemy lines to Jaffna, and on to a departing ship.

'We all loved her. During the shooting of the film two years ago, she was idolised by all of us. Most young men would have gone through hell just to be near her.

And a couple of times, I was lucky enough to be able to drive her to her hotel in my taxi. Don't ask me how many times I've seen the film! I'm absolutely sure it was her.'

'But just what do you think happened?'

'I don't know. It's as if the military had her under their control and had the power to bring her back to life and torture her to death over and over again.'

'Where did you get such an absurd idea?'

'The military hates her. The army had a say in the shooting of the film and the ministry of war asked for some changes in the script. But when the film was released, there was a lot of ill feeling because the terrorist had been changed into a brave, courageous freedom fighter and the Sinhalese officers into villains. They've not allowed the film to be shown to this day in Sri Lanka. If they could . . . ' he hesitated and glanced at me, 'if they could, they would, just to get their revenge.'

'Could what?'

'Kill her. Kill her over and over again.'

'That's mad!'

'I'm a devout Buddhist, Mr Kirk. I believe in rebirth, but whatever this is, it's something unnatural, something wicked and evil. And it happened right here in this city.'

Hadn't Andrew mentioned something about rebirth? No, he had asked: *Do you believe in the resurrection of the flesh?* What could he have meant by that?

'You don't believe me?'

I shook my head. 'No.'

I should have known then. There were a few strange stories in the newspapers, but no one believed them, except for those who knew what was going on. The facts were quite evident at the time. The information was there at our disposal. The data just had to be retrieved and classified. True, there were several sharks lurking in the infopool, snapping at anyone who tried to get information about someone called Cecil Roughtrade. A computer freak like Andrew Baldenham could have broken the code and fooled them, but he and I had been away from earth too long. In outer space, any news of immediate interest from Rome or London was viewed with an astronomic perspective.

In the end, however, they fooled him.

2

The Roar of the Surf

The sun crept up the trunks, nested in the plumage of the tree tops and shone around the well-rounded testicles of the coconut palm.

I stepped onto the balcony, felt the sensation of concrete under the soles of my feet and scratched my chest. I discovered six or seven new bites. Six months in a space suit or in the well-tempered sterile atmosphere of the troop room made any immediate contact with nature seem an elementary experience. However, after five months of work in Nanguneri, I was sick and tired of the damn mosquitoes. The awe-inspiring view of the universe was better than being at the mercy of one of its thousands of pests.

The chirping of the crickets was deafening and the monotonous singsong of the fishermen could be heard from the beach. They had cast their large net in a wide circle across the bay as they did every morning at sunrise. It took them hours to pull it in and set up the thick coir ropes into black-brown mounds, systematically covering the white sand of the bay from one end to the other.

'Pimpernay – everyday. Pimpernay – everyday . . . ' Fifty men and their soul-destroying, tedious movements. Before long, they would clamour loudly as they fought over the scanty catch – a couple of bigger fish, a few shellfish and the usual small ones. This method of catching fish had been a tradition in this country for thousands of years. However, the haul had become appallingly meagre over the past half-century as pollution had destroyed the spawning grounds in the coral reefs. In addition, out at sea, the modern haul vessels of the Japanese fleet ruthlessly cleaned the very depths of the ocean for hard currency. However, no one ever thought of controlling the prolific birthrate of these people.

'Pimpernay – every day. Pimpernay – everyday.' The bow of the net tightened almost imperceptibly.

I looked at my watch. It was only half-past eight. Several soldiers were drilling on the grounds of the military base, the former park of the luxury hotel Ashok Beach. They were crawling through the high, unruly grass of what had once been the lawn of a golf course, holding automatic rifles in their fists and working their way ahead on their elbows. In spite of the fresh, cool morning air, their sand-coloured uniforms were dampened with sweat. From time to time an officer's loud commands could be heard above the sound of the surf and the singsong of the fishermen. I went outside onto the balcony and walked the length of it, examining the façade of the Sea Queen for bullet holes from the gunfight the night before. I found none. The doors of the cave-like rooms stood open. Now and again, a half-naked figure lay on a bed; probably some hotel employee who had retreated to an empty room in order not to let himself in for some job early in the morning.

The noise of an engine could be heard approaching nearer and nearer. A combat helicopter skimmed over the tops of the palm trees and landed on the former parking lot of the Ashok Beach Hotel. The whop-whop-whop of the propeller blades died down and stopped. The singsong of the fishermen filled the still air once again. I wiped the sweat from my chest and went back into my room. I lay down on my bed, enjoying the stream of air from the fan up on the ceiling, and stared at the shadowy whirl of its blades. The machine clung with unflagging stubbornness to one of the beams. Occasionally, a puff of sawdust escaped into the moving air. With the painstaking help of the termites, the fan would, at some time or other, succeed in tearing itself away and would plunge down on some unsuspecting guest, slashing him to pieces.

I crossed my arms behind my head. We had been stranded for days in Kovalam, the former luxury resort to the far south. Everything had been delayed, as was always the case in such countries. The antenna station of Nanguneri – Sunbird 3 supplied it with energy from outer space – should have been linked to the network in September, but some political agitators had stirred up trouble among the peasants and had convinced them that everything within a radius of a hundred miles would be grilled by the microwaves from space if the receiving antenna were put into operation. It didn't do any good to explain that the reception was laser-controlled and that, at the slightest deviation in the focused beam of the microwaves, the receiving antenna would automatically be disconnected from the orbital station. They had visions of horror – steaming steaks sliding off the ribs of their sacred cows; themselves and their children wiped out completely; and their land not only consumed by fire but contaminated forever. What they didn't understand was that energy was as necessary as rain. Only rich landowners could afford diesel oil for the water pumps, while the rice on the village land rotted. This was exactly what the landowners and political agitators had hoped for. They incited the peasants to rob the trucks transporting our materials, and to set fire to the workers' quarters. The army was then called in. There were a few deaths – the same old story.

I had decided to spend my vacation with Andrew in Sri Lanka, before we were to report to NASA again. Andrew knew the island well. He had been there a couple of times as a student – tourism had been popular then. I didn't feel like going back to Portland. It would be foggy, damp and cold in Oregon at that time of the year. Ruth was probably living in our apartment and I didn't want to see her. We had separated on bad terms and the longer I thought about it, the more lousy I felt about the role I had played in the whole affair.

I sat up and looked around. Patches of light flickered over the ceiling like transparent living tissues, magnified. Something had woken me in the night. Was it someone calling? A scream? I stepped out on to the balcony to see. The surf shimmered white between the trunks of the trees. The sand on the beach sparkled as the water flowed back. The shadowy hands of the palm trees were submerged in a blaze of twinkling stars. The night was moonless. Suddenly, about three hundred metres from the shore, I saw a flare of muzzle flash, heard the roar of a machine gun and, at that very instant, bullets frazzled through the bushes and shrubbery in front of the hotel. I tried to protect myself by crouching behind the shoulder-high balustrade of the balcony. One of the bullets ricocheted somewhere and shrieked up into the night sky. Lights went on in the hotel.

'Put the lights out!' I howled, crawling, completely terrified, back into the room. Obviously, no one understood me. I slammed the door behind me, even though I realized that wood would have no more resistance to a steel-core bullet than the material of my pyjamas. Using the wall as protection, I peered through the open window. The fighting had now moved further to the west. The line of bullets stretched like a chain of fireflies to the top of the cliff on which the Ashok Beach Hotel stood. They had obviously been woken by the noise and had opened fire in return. Streams of orange-coloured fireflies poured into the ocean. The noise of a motorboat with a powerful engine rose and faded as it reached the open sea. Far too late, a signal rocket was set off, covering the bay for a second in a pale, sickly light. Birds were scared into flight and a pair of terror-stricken monkeys screeched. Then, the night sank even deeper into the darkness. The nightmare was over.

I pulled the sheet up between my legs, spreading it over my body as if it could give me much-needed protection, and tried to calm my racing heart. This incident was typical of the inexplicable, but permanant, guerrilla wars in the countries of the Third World. Exhausting their strength and energy and wastefully consuming ammunition, they'd stage nightly hit-and-run skirmishes and occasional acts of piracy. With a carefully directed raid, the Sinhalese, as the Buddhists of Sri Lanka called themselves, could have destroyed the antenna station of Nanguneri in a matter of minutes and, in so doing, ruin sixteen months of work of German, French and Japanese companies. Naturally, fear of triggering off an atomic attack on the part of India prevented this. Besides, one day they might profit from this station and its cheap energy from outer space, so they did nothing more than provoke India with small gibes.

It took me a long time to get to sleep again and when I finally did, terror crawled through the labyrinth of my dreams like a dark, blood-stained worm.

'Listen, Peter!' Andrew said and pointed with his crutch to the open door of the balcony. 'We've got to get out of here!'

At the back of the room, three dark-skinned soldiers in battle dress had taken up their position. They held their machine guns pointing upwards, barrels pressed against their chests. I sat up in bed with great difficulty, clenching my teeth and with terrible pains in my groin. The nurse, who was supporting Andrew, gave me a provocative wink. She was an Indian woman in her mid-thirties or forties. Her smile exposed a set of rotten teeth. She let the tip of her tongue whip quickly back and forth over them. Outside in the corridor, crossfire could be heard and soldiers rushed to take up their positions.

'I've let everything run through the computer again,' Andrew said. The pants of his pyjamas were stained right through with blood. He pointed to the door with his crutch. 'There's no other way out, Peter,' he said. The nurse held him tightly, nodding all the while at me in an inviting manner. 'We'll have to brave it now.' He carelessly wiped away the blood that gushed out of his mouth and nose with the sleeve of his pyjama. 'You just have to repeat over and over to yourself that they couldn't possibly want to harm you.'

'Okay,' I answered and started towards the door. It took me a long time and was excruciatingly painful. At last I reached the door and opened it. The soldiers raised their guns and opened fire.

I awoke gasping for breath and bathed in sweat. The blades of the fan above me stood still. Another power failure – there was one every few hours.

The dream was very disturbing. It haunted me again and again, always the same horrible desperate situation.

And I also knew the woman dressed as a nurse. She was the one who cleaned our room and helped in the kitchen. She was a widow. 'She ought to have been cremated at her dead husband's side,' Mr Lain, the manager of the Sea Queen, said, pursing his thick lips to light a cigarette. 'The suttee used to be a custom in India, Mr Kirk,' he blew smoke into my face, 'and it's no longer banned today.' He blinked his eyes at me and bent over the counter. 'She runs after every foreigner,' he whispered in a confidential voice. 'Why don't you take advantage before it's too late, Mr Kirk. Mr Baldenham is not at all shy in that respect.' He made a fist and gestured suggestively.

I didn't bother answering. More than likely Andrew had already slept with her.

I was brushing my teeth when the light in the bathroom went on and the fan started up with a screech. I decided to shave before the power system broke down again. I had trouble seeing myself in the mirror as it was scratched and worn. The long feelers of a cockroach appeared over the edge. Warily, it tested its position. Disgusted, I pulled the plug out of the wobbly socket.

I was just about to go down to breakfast when Andrew appeared in the doorway.

'The water's not working again,' he declared sullenly, and scratched his bald, sunburned head, scaling off some of the skin.

'They turn the water off at nine – you know that.'

'But it's not nine yet!'

'Tell that to Mr Lain – not me!'

'My God, you're in a bad mood. Heh, you're not jealous, are you?'

'No, I'm not.'

'Do you know how old she is?'

'Between thirty and sixty. Judging from her teeth, she's more like sixty.'

'You're wrong. She's twenty-four and she's an artist.'

'Congratulations! Didn't you hear the shooting last night?'

'Yes, but I was busy.' He grinned complacently.

'It's no joke, Andrew. That was the second surprise attack this week. We should have them give us a room on the ground floor. They're more protected.'

'These rooms,' he said with an expansive gesture that included the room and its dirty stained walls, which at some time or other had been painted a light green, 'are the suites of the Sea Queen. They are reserved for very privileged guests. Look at this spectacular view of the ocean and smell the fresh ocean breeze!'

All I could think of was the smell of garlic and rotten fish, which had seeped up from the kitchen until long after midnight. 'Those holes down there were the dens of hippies for almost half a century!' He turned up his nose in disgust. 'And believe me, Peter, no manager of this time-honoured hotel ever thought of buying new mattresses.' He pulled the sheets off my bed. 'However, I see that they're not much better up here.'

I looked in disgust at the mattress.

'Every mattress has its own history,' he said as if he were giving a lecture to members of a commission.

'Especially hotel mattresses. They can be compared with maps. Just look at it. Bed-wetters and soldiers of fortune have mapped out the coastal areas. Graffiti maniacs have named the landmarks, especially in the centre of the continent.' He pointed to a seminal fluid stain in the middle of the mattress. Somebody had outlined it with a red felt-tipped pen in the form of a heart. Above the heart were the words – I FUCKED HER HERE. Some joker had crossed out the HER and had written HIM beside it. Monuments of long-forgotten triumphs, hippie happiness.

I yanked the mattress out of its frame and turned it over. Another hemisphere of the same world. Continents of nightmares and passion.

'What an awful mess! I'll have a talk with Mr Lain.'

Andrew grinned. 'Good luck!'

The singsong of the fishermen had stopped. They had pulled in their net.

'I'm going down to the beach,' I said.

*   *   *

They had hauled in a dead body with their net. A young boy, sixteen years old at the most. He was dressed in khaki shorts and a short-sleeved military shirt which had come unbuttoned to reveal his lean, light-skinned young breast. Small, shiny silver fish fluttered over his body like poplar leaves in the wind. His hair and mouth were full of sand and there was a bullet hole just above his heart. A thin thread of rust-coloured liquid ran from his water-soaked flesh.

A jeep rushed up over the sand and came screeching to a halt. Soldiers in battle-dress jumped out, shoved the fishermen to one side with the butts of their rifles and yanked the body out of the net. They made no effort to free the body from the net; just cut the net and dragged the body to the feet of the officer. The dying fish fell from the breast of the young man like scales from a fragile suit of armour and created a thin silver path on the wet sand.

The officer started to question the fishermen. They babbled away excitedly, moving their toothless mouths. Hate filled their dark eyes at the sight of the dead enemy, but also a trace of fear. Someone kicked the body and spat on it. The officer pushed the body back with his cane, gently, but with force.

'Who are you?' he asked me.

I told him my name.

'Go back to your hotel!' he said in a quiet, but commanding voice. 'This is a military matter.'

I had a good look at the catch. Hardly more than a couple of dozen fish. They floundered pitifully to death. The fishermen were more interested in the young man. His face, covered in sand, seemed to have started to decompose – earth to earth – his wound had run dry. One last perishing fish clung to his body like a silver leaf.

The officer looked at me. His mirrored sunglasses were impenetrable. He impatiently flicked his cane against his boot. I turned around and made my way obediently back to the hotel.

3

The Sad Elephant

'The filthy pirate,' the manager of the Sea Queen said, shrugging his shoulders. He continued cleaning his betel-brown teeth.

'He wore a uniform.'

'The filthy pirate in uniform then, Mr Kirk. They are all gangsters. The Sinhalese. The paw of the lion they call themselves. What a joke. The Tamil tiger will tear the mangy lion to pieces and throw its remains to the seas.'

A calendar hung on the wall behind him with a picture of Ganesha, the elephant god, his enormous behind crushing a rat. The elephant's red eyes were filled with malice and almost blinded by fly-speck. December 18, 2016. They were already in the 52nd century in this country. Colourful garlands framed the year 5116 near the fat, left-hand hind leg of the elephant god.

'When will the airship arrive?'

'In two or three days. Who knows, perhaps even tomorrow.'

'That's what you told us two or three days ago, Mr Lain.'

He shrugged his shoulders. 'The wind is coming from the southwest. Rare for this time of year. The ship won't make much progress against the wind. Bombay is far away. It'll arrive some day, don't worry.'

'Can I have a new mattress, Mr Lain?'

He looked at me, unable to understand. On the wall, the Ganesha was grinning wickedly. 'Listen here, Mr Kirk. I know you've done an awful lot for my country and I would be glad to do anything for you in return, but today such things are not easy to . . .'

'What would a new one cost?'

Mr Lain lowered his silken eyelashes to the pocket calculator lying among the faded registration forms and the badly printed newspapers on the reception desk and began to calculate. 'Two hundred dollars, Mr Kirk.'

I gave him two hundred dollar pieces.

'I'll send the boy into town with the bus that leaves at noon, Mr Kirk. You'll have your mattress this evening.'

'Thank you, Mr Lain.'

'Doesn't Mr Baldenham need a new mattress?'

'No, Mr Baldenham doesn't need a new mattress.'

Mr Lain began to grin, opened his mouth to utter a shrill shriek not at all in line with his soft-spoken nature. 'I understand,' he snorted and burst out laughing.

The boy had not yet returned although it was almost midnight. I moved to one of the rooms on the ground floor. The balcony ran round the whole building and had a high balustrade. Thick bushes blocked the view of the bay, but provided additional protection. I didn't want to take the risk of being hit by some stray bullet, whether pirate or patriot. With a shudder of disgust, I spread two sheets over the hemisphere on the mattress and stretched out to rest over countries and oceans, heights and depths of love, and fell fast asleep.

Sometime during the night, two combat helicopters landed at the base, but started off shortly after. At daybreak they returned home. They had fired off all their rockets.

*   *   *

The airship didn't arrive the next day, nor the next. And the boy never showed up again, either. 'I told you it wasn't easy, Mr Kirk,' the manager said. However, I was sure the devil had pocketed the money himself and sent the boy home to keep him out of sight until our departure.

The following day – there had been a storm during the night with a real downpour – we were sitting on the terrace having our breakfast when suddenly, we heard a great commotion. Children were splashing through the large puddles in the street calling out excitedly, 'The elephant! The elephant!' The whole village seemed to be up. They all ran to the west side of the bay – beyond the area that was off-limits to all but the military.

Mr Lain hurried to where we were sitting on the terrace, spread open his arms and announced, 'Didn't I tell you that it would come today?'

We jumped up to join the crowd. Drops of water fell from the palm trees. The air had the fresh smell of grass and franchipanis in bloom. The puddles reflected the grey, rain-filled sky and – we couldn't believe our eyes – the airship actually descended from this same sky. It swept down out of the clouds – giant, wet and glistening!

Under its powerful, protective belly was a long thin gondola made out of aluminium and plastic, four storeys high. It was a combination of passenger ship, freight container and pullman car. On the top, at the front, was the glassed-in cockpit; behind, on its roof, passengers sat closely packed together between boxes, baskets and bundles in the shade of the balloon-like body. The flag of Singapore – a white half crescent moon and five white stars in a red field on a white-red background – was painted on the snubbed nose of the machine and at the bottom of it were the words:

SULTAN AHMET
EFRAIM HASIM SDN. BHD.
AIR & SEA TRANSPORTS

The airship manoeuvred its nose towards the fence of a latticed tower, its propellers growling. A man stood on the platform of the tower signalling with pennants. An anchor line was shot down and fastened tightly. Half-naked figures climbed along the railing of the gondola, lines were lowered and secured. Whistles and commands rang out and the hawsers were eased out and pulled over rollers. With the same singsong with which they had hauled in their net, the fishermen, who had hurried to help, pulled the balloon down from the sky until the gondala landed with a crunch on the sand and was tied down firmly. All of a sudden so many passengers poured out of the ship that it literally seemed to explode. They were immediately surrounded by women and children with baskets full of fruit and nuts. Before long, the beach resembled a gypsy camp.

The bull-like airship filled with helium was completely covered over with dark, glittering solar batteries. As the four gondala engines at the bow and stern of the ship had been eased out, it now looked like one of those elephants covered in mirrors sold in all sizes to the tourists from the USA, Europe and Japan. However, with its dark glistening harness under the sombre sky, pregnant with rain, it now looked like a very sad elephant.

I waited until the paymaster of the Sultan Ahmet had paid the fishermen who had helped to haul the airship down, and then asked him what the fare to Colombo would cost. He strapped his embroidered leather pouch, from which he had taken the rupees, to his belt. He sized me up, assessing just how much I was worth, and stroked his stately grey handlebar moustache. He was a Sikh, almost six feet tall, his uncut hair hidden under his turban.

'Three thousand dollars.'

'For a berth?'

'No, for a bed.'

'And on the roof?'

'Two thousand rupees. Off limits for whites.'

It was natural for whites to be charged many times over what the natives were charged, but this was really steep. Not that it made any difference to us. Our travelling expenses were reimbursed by NASA anyway, but it would make a big dent in our cash. American Express was a thing of the past, along with mass tourism. Payment was in cash – in silver hundred dollar pieces issued by the government-owned bank in Singapore – and we still had two months of vacation to go.

'Without money, you're an outcast,' the American ambassador in New Delhi had warned us, 'and an outcast here is untouchable.' There was also a deep-seated aversion to anything or anyone American. The USA had let the countries of the Third World fend for themselves during the famine that took place at the turn of the century and had invested $500 billion in weapons in space instead. Of course, progress had been made in outer space by EFOS*, but for four hundred million people, the cheap energy from outer space came too late.

I booked two tickets for the Sultan Ahmet and counted sixty silverlings into the large brown hand of the paymaster. He ripped two colourful tickets from a block and handed them to me with the condescension of a seller of indulgences.

'We leave at three o'clock in the afternoon.'

I strolled over to Andrew. He was standing by one of

---

*Energy From Outer Space

the gondola engines that was being eased out and was watching the flight mechanics fit the driving muscle into place. During the day, the airship used electrical power from its solar batteries – at night it had to use muscle power.

They hoisted the muscle – half the size of an ox and at least ten hundred-weights heavy – with a pulley block out of the temperature-controlled aluminium container filled with a nutrient fluid. They then washed it down with warm water and lowered it into the operating tub where the gristly outgrowths of its blunt side were stuck tightly to a strong steel frame, while the smooth side with its ligaments was joined to the crank shaft. Three of these muscles set one propeller into motion. A round blue sign the size of a plate was tattooed into the whitish skin: HITACHI BIOTECH. Living mammoth muscle tissue produced by means of back-breeding, millions of tons of which were grown in Japanese bio-laboratories, cheaper and more efficient than AMERICAN BISON and viable for up to one year. After the one year period it was released for consumption – providing those eating it had strong-enough teeth.

The mechanics clamped off the flow of blood from the regeneration container and joined the arteries to the supply network of the gondola. When all three muscles were attached and connected, the pulse-generator electrodes were plugged into the rudimentary nerve cord. A microprocessor controlled the pulse by means of an exact firing order, while a sensor in the bloodstream monitored the amount of synthetic adrenaline and the blood pressure of each bio-unit. A test run followed: the muscles tightened in their frame and set the crank shaft into motion. Suddenly, a plastic artery broke itself loose, spraying the men with blood. They repaired the cause of the trouble and laughed as they wiped their faces with the tips of their turbans. Then the stampede of those powerful primitive animals set forth over imaginary tundras with electronically induced flight reflexes and chemically-controlled fear and stamina. A well-cared for, well-fed and well-trained Hitachi-mammoth, pumped full of adrenaline, can last up to thirty hours.

One of the mechanics said something to me, but I couldn't understand him. He grinned.

'What's he saying?' I asked Andrew.

'He wants to know whether you need a blood transfusion – you look so pale.'

'Thank you!' I called to him over the muscles, which were moving with more and more suppleness.

When we returned to the Sea Queen, dozens of new guests were already waiting at the reception. The whole place smelled of sweat and garlic.

'Mr Kirk!' the manager called above the racket. 'Your mattress has arrived!'

And, believe it or not, there it was lying against the wall covered with ugly green and blue flowers, chastely packed in plastic foil.

Some of the new guests looked at me strangely.

'Why did it take the boy three days to get it?'

'He had to visit his family in town,' he called apologetically. 'When's the poor boy a chance to visit his family? You must try to understand, Mr Kirk.'

The same guests were indignant at the fact that I could possibly have anything against the poor boy visiting his family. I made a hasty retreat, shrugging my shoulders, went to my room and packed my bag.

Andrew then came to my room, sat down on my bed and sighed. 'How can I tell her I'm leaving this afternoon?'

'You were never one to be lost for words!'

'I feel like a heel.'

'Then why don't you stop fooling around with every woman in sight? Why don't you take her with you to

Colombo. She could have her belated widow's suttee there. They make short work of Tamils there.'

'You are so unfair.'

'Really – you don't say?'

'My God!' Andrew roared. 'I'm fifteen years older than you, Pete, but sometimes you act like a cantankerous old man with nothing more to expect from life. I know you're having trouble with your wife and that your marriage is on the rocks, although you've never mentioned a word about it. I can see there's something wrong. You don't need to pamper your hurt pride for months on end. When something like that happens, both parties are usually guilty.'

'You don't understand!'

'But I do understand, much more than you think, Pete.'

I grabbed my bag and rushed downstairs to pay the bill.

Naturally, I had become suspicious, had even spied on her occasionally, but without any concrete results. I took a few precautions before I left for outer space as I presumed that Ruth would have no scruples about sleeping with her lover in our bed during my absence. That's my wife, I kept repeating over and over to myself. I stared at the TV screen and was fascinated by the passion, the tenderness and fervour with which she could love someone else. Once, they fell out of bed together and probably continued making love on the floor, but the load switch stopped the videotape until the weight of the two bodies activated the scale again. Some kind of interference rippled across the screen with a sawlike pattern and distorted the image of the copulating bodies. Their movements, separated by a jagged silver glimmering ribbon, seemed to flounder in an absurd way.

That's my wife, I kept whining over and over again in a nauseating mixture of self-righteousness and damaged pride. My hands ached, so I held onto the arms of my chair. It was cold in the room as I had forgotten to close the window again.

'Why is it so cold in here?' she called from the doorway and, with one of her typical movements, shook the hair out of her face and took off her trenchcoat. 'I've just bought us some delicious food. I'll cook you something fantastic. I imagine you could do with a decent meal after all this time.'

I couldn't stop the videotape. A tanned back, heaving loins, delicate hands caressing the back of a head, closed eyes in a tender face, eternal ecstasies, disheveled blonde curls, lips greedily seeking an ear, a mouth, loins accelerating their rhythm.

I heard her pant, groan, an almost absurd croaking scream, a deep throaty sound – harrowing, almost painful. Then she began to strike at me with her fists, hitting me on my head and shoulders. This snapped me out of my paralysed state. I jumped up and held her wrists tightly. She kicked and tugged like a mad woman in a wild rage and with the tips of her shoes hit my shin bones. 'You're a real swine!' she screamed. 'How can you be such a swine?'

'That's what I wanted to ask you.'

'You self-righteous monster! You pervert!'

While she was trying to tear herself away, her head lay for a moment on my chest – hardly a moment. My lips touched her hair. It was still wet from the rain and I inhaled its fragrance. This is what I had longed for for months on end while in orbit. I could never exactly remember her hair, only knew that I loved it. This moment alone, this half second, made me almost prepared to forget everything and not only erase the videotape, but dismiss it from my memory forever.

However, the moment passed. We obviously couldn't hold on to it – hold on to one another.

I drove that same evening to our cabin by the ocean. It belonged to our club and all the members had a key. No one was there. I lit the fire. It had rained all night. I finally fell asleep to the sound of raindrops beating on the roof of my car parked under the fir trees in front of the cabin.

Next morning the weather had cleared up. I jogged along the beach for a couple of hours, striding along with large steps. After the suffocating closeness of the orbital station, I always have this great need to be free, to leave space behind – to have the feeling of pushing the earth away from me with every step, of setting the earth into motion. I jogged at a slow trot along the beach. Shells crunched underfoot, fragments of time. My lungs were bursting with air. The waves of the Pacific rolled towards me out of nowhere, broke near my feet, hissing back in a whisper. Completely exhausted, I stretched out on the damp sand. Its coolness was refreshing. The anger I had felt all night long like a large, heavy stone in the cage of my breast was gone. The pain ebbed with every breath. I opened my eyes and saw a piece of blue sky directly above me through a hole in the clouds. And suddenly I felt as if I were lying with my back against a cold surface and looking down into an abyss – the slightest movement and I would plunge to the depths. Every astronaut who has walked outdoors in space has this feeling. I closed my eyes and waited until I was sure that I was really lying on my back and could stand up.

'I didn't know that you were such a crafty voyeur,' Danny said, grinning with relish at the thought. He scraped the rest of the rice and sauce together and stuffed it into his mouth with a quick movement. He then sank back into his chair and reached for his napkin.

'That videotape is worth its weight in gold.' He had spilled some food on his tie and was dabbing the spot with his napkin. His fat face was red from the simple effort of looking down. 'You'll have absolutely no alimony to pay with all this evidence against her.' He sniggered, amused at the thought, and patted me on the arm solicitously. A button of his shirt had burst under the strain of his stomach, revealing a pale hairy piece of skin that fascinated me. I suddenly felt physically ill at the thought of handing him over the videotape.

'Who's going to see the tape, anyway?'

'I will, of course, as your lawyer. The judge, probably the members of the jury and perhaps an expert witness.'

Expert witness? His stomach bounced when he laughed.

'Are you having second thoughts? I tell you that tape is worth its weight in gold. It will save you a lot of money.'

'What a shame.'

'What do you mean?'

'I threw it into the ocean.'

His face fell. 'Haven't you got a copy?'

'No, no copy.'

As I got up to leave, I couldn't help noticing the headlines of a newspaper that someone had left on the next table.

ALLEGED DOUBLE
OF THE KIDNAPPED NOBEL PRIZE
WINNER
MURDERED

The man who insisted that he was the Nobel Prize winner, Giuseppe Torre, was found shot to death

in a New York hotel. He had been kidnapped
months earlier. Mrs Torre confirms that the man is
not her husband.

Newspaper headlines have never really interested me
all that much. That was always one of my mistakes.

4

The Mirror of the Ocean

'Mr Kirk, Sir! Mr Kirk!' a cawing voice called after we had already gone through passport control. 'Your mattress, Mr Kirk!'

It was the boy from the Sea Queen. He had actually dragged the mattress down to the launch pad.

'It's yours to keep as a present,' I called back. 'Make yourself a lovely world!'

'What should I make, Mr Kirk?'

'Aw, nothing. Sleep well, that's all. Pleasant dreams.'

'Thanks, Mr Kirk. Have a good trip!'

Half an hour later, the ropes were unfastened and hauled in and the Sultan Ahmet rose into the air. The muscles of our galley mammoth tightened in anticipation, the propellers rumbled, thrusting the airship towards the south-east.

Andrew ordered a beer from the cabin steward, raised his glass and looked sadly back at the coast. 'Excuse me, I didn't really mean to bawl you out a little while ago,' he said.

'Forget it. You were right after all.'

We stared out of the thin plastic window of our cabin. Under us, night was gathering over the land.

I slept badly and awoke, startled, time and again as I was convinced that the airship had got out of control. The slight swaying movement of the gondola irritated me. Besides, the berth was too small to be able to stretch my legs and too narrow to lie down with my knees pulled up. I pushed the small window open a bit and let the cool air of the night into the cabin. It was unusually quiet with only the muffled groaning of the balloon's rigging, the singing of the wind in the lines and braces and the hushed whir of the propellers, eerily driven by an electronic herd.

The morning dawned. A sailor, who was squatting in the window of one of the gondola engines, a blanket slung around his shoulders to keep out the cold, waved to me. I waved back.

I got out of my berth quietly and stood barefoot on the thin straw mat which carpeted the cubicle. Andrew was sleeping soundly. I looked at him in the semi-darkness. His thick brown moustache hung sadly over the corner of his slightly open mouth. In spite of his becoming bald and greying at the temples, he looked surprisingly young. Sleep had ironed out almost all the wrinkles on his forehead and around the corners of his eyes. There was something boyish about him in spite of his fifty-four years. He was a small, wiry man with just a hint of a beer belly. It didn't go with the rest of his figure at all. Dressed in bleached-out jeans, a sports shirt, a shabby leather jacket and worn-out running shoes, it was hard to believe that he was one of the top computer special-ists on the EFOS team.

'Computer software,' he was fond of correcting. 'I'm only interested in the software, not the wiring. Don't know anything about it.' Even as a teenager he had shaken up Telenet, as it was called then, and had scared the authorities out of their wits because he was able to break every code in the book. Later, he had studied under Alan Garfinkel at UCLA and made a name for himself in the field of chaos research. He was a deter-minist and considered the randomist theory an error in reasoning, even after their victory in the philosophical confrontation that followed.

Andrew had joined the EFOS team fairly late, about AD 2010 I had already been with them for six years when he started. He refused to discuss what he had done before. 'I fought with the randomists and they won. It was a secret mission for the government and nothing came of it, but we had to swear that we wouldn't say a thing. So stop trying to squeeze any information out of me, boys! Please try to understand.'

'A bomb?'

'It would've turned into the greatest thing the world had ever seen. We could've bombed hunger out of the world.'

'And how long were you with them?'

'Twelve years.'

'A hell of a long time for a project that was put on ice!'

'We were just unlucky. Basic research brought results that were against us. But I'm convinced they used the wrong mathematics in their calculations.'

When Andrew started at Sunbird 3, I was placed under him as telemetry engineer. He was responsible for working out the programs for the solar satellite – a laser-controlled antenna alignment system – and had to decide in what order and for how long the satellite would supply the antenna fields between Pakistan and Japan, Zimbabwe and Australia from its slightly swaying, but stationary, orbit. I was responsible for providing him with data on this with the accuracy of plus/minus four inches, to 22,245 miles.

Nanguneri in Southern India was the last ground station to be tested and put into operation. Sunbird 3 was already in full working order. Now, it was our task to prepare Sunbird 4 for operation. In the meantime, between Port-au-Prince and Montevideo, Nouachott and Swakopmund, the antenna fields were being set up.

I got dressed and went down to the second-class passenger deck. The room was crammed with seats like a

charter jet of the last century. Most of the passengers
were sleeping with blankets or had their spacious robes
wrapped around them. A child whimpered. The mother
rocked it, staring at me. The sliding windows were all
closed. It smelled of vomit and dirty diapers.

I went to the front and took the stairs down to the bar.
Two men in white burnooses leaned at the bar, poured
themselves coffee in faded plastic saucers and sipped
noisily, conversing with one another in Arabic. One of
them had scars on his face. It looked as if someone had
hacked at it with a hoe blade. He gave me a friendly
nod, revealing a fortune in gold. I smiled back and
ordered coffee from the barkeeper, who was washing
cups in a tiny plastic pail.

'Not Nescafé,' he declared proudly, and poured my
coffee. 'Malacca Coffee.' He shoved a giant bowl of
sugar my way.

I drank the hot, thin brew, paid and climbed three
flights to the roof of the passenger deck. Goods and
baggage covered every inch of the floor and the deck
passengers, muffled against the cold, were sleeping
among them under the protective belly of the elephant.

We were about two thousand feet above sea-level.
The weather had cleared up. The morning air was cool.
Sailors, dressed in nothing but loin cloths and turbans,
boarded the ship to polish the solar cells clean. Their
small brown feet clutched the footrests of the rope-
ladder. One of the men stopped halfway up the ladder
and relieved himself, producing an impeccable para-
bolic curve which lost itself to the depths. Towards the
east, the ocean lay like a fluted metal surface. Light
began to fill the sky. Far ahead, we could make out a
light streak, like a pale garland pinned to the horizon –
the coastline of Ceylon.

The sky filled with light. Dark, big-bellied clouds, like
the small, fast caravel ships of former times, sailed
towards us. Their booms and planks were shredded by

our propellers and flew away like smoke. This interplay between light and dark became even more colourful. A pale green gave way to a strong vermilion, the upper clouds reflected a red glow, their fire catching the upper edges of the lower clouds, which brightened to warmer tones, then to yellow, and ultimately to white. The sun had risen.

A long shrill whistle could be heard on the deck. The heads of the travellers emerged from the depths of their coats and covers, brown faces, shaven heads, white beards, toothless yawning mouths. Hand signals were sent back and forth between the deck and the four gondola engines. The captain had the drive shifted over to solar energy in order to save the energy of the bio-motors. The adrenaline was stopped, sedatives were pumped into the bloodstream, the nerve impulses gradually slackened. The strong muscles relaxed and stopped altogether. The trembling flanks were filled with oxygen-enriched blood in order to wash out the slag formation, while the driving mechanism was disconnected and the electric engines were put into operation. The propellers began to rotate faster again. Suddenly, a knocking sound was heard above the steady hum of the propellers. A weapon-laden combat helicopter poised in mid-air and, about seventy feet above our flying altitude, took up its firing position. A fierce-looking lion was painted on its side, marigold-coloured on a brown background. In its right paw it was triumphantly holding something that looked part-carving knife, part-sceptre. I saw the dark faces of the men under their steel helmets, impenetrable faces. Men, who at the drop of a command, would be willing to kill anything in sight. I had the urge to release my electronic brass knuckles to jam their board electronics, but that would have probably set off a catastrophe.

Our captain held a megaphone to his lips and called over to them. The helicopter pilot answered via a loudspeaker. A dispute ensued which sounded like the gobbling of mad turkeys. Once, I thought I heard them mention the name Baldenham, but I wasn't sure. Finally, the helicopter veered off and disappeared to the south-east, while the Sultan Ahmet continued on its course along the coast.

'Visitors just paid you a call.' Andrew was eating his breakfast. He glanced up and looked at me in surprise. 'I think they asked for you.'

'Bull shit!' he said, mopping up his fried eggs with the flat Indian bread. 'Have you had any breakfast?' he asked.

'A coffee, that's all.'

'Sit down!'

Five Buddhist monks were sitting nearby. They had round, shorn heads and well-fed bodies dressed in flowing, orange-coloured garments, one foot curled up comfortably under their behinds. Theirs was a friendly, satisfied and well-fed religion which had enjoyed world-wide popularity before the turn of the millennium, even in western countries.

'Have you ever heard of the name Cecil Roughtrade?' Andrew asked.

'Roughtrade?'

'He was the brainpower behind the determinists in the chaos controversy of the '90s.'

'That was before my time.'

'I was one of his assistants on the MIDAS project. Like him, I really believed in the project. I still believe in it, even today.'

'MIDAS?'

Lost in thought, he tapped his lips as if he wanted to force himself into silence and said in a whisper, 'Molecular Integrating and Digital Assembling System – the basis for Multimanna. A Moby, as we used to say, a fantastic project and cuspy, mathematically absolutely

okay, even if the Bogons, those idiot randomists, were
of the opposite opinion.'

'And what's it good for?'

He grunted and resolutely shovelled his breakfast
into his mouth.

'Read this!' he said, and handed me a crumpled
Washington Post that someone had left behind. It was
dated December 13th – more than a week old. Andrew
pointed with a nod of his head to the headlines.

RODESTROM'S DOUBLE DEAD

*(A.P.) Following a short, serious illness, the man who
had maintained that he was the well-known physicist
and Nobel prize winner Bengt Rodestrom, died last
Friday in a London hospital. Rodestrom had made a
name for himself in ULT (Ultra Low Temperature)
research at the turn of the millennium. As a result of his
research, the storage capacity of crystals could be
enlarged one hundredfold. Rodestrom and his colleague,
Mario Battani, had received the Nobel prize for Physics
in 2004 for the project. Mr Rodestrom was not available
for comment. The professor had retired to the seclusion of
a Danish island, called Samso, after almost dying of a
heart attack at a Congress for Physicists in Manila eight
years ago. An autopsy performed on the corpse in a
London Hospital revealed important discrepancies in
spite of the unbelievable resemblance to Rodestrom: the
man in question was six to eight years younger than
Rodestrom with a complete set of teeth and a deformation
of the left ankle, congenital according to the doctors.
Also, there was no trace of his ever having had a heart
attack. His organs revealed a series of deformities and
malfunctions that were more than likely the cause of his
death. One of the doctors, Dr Shaw, was quoted as*

*saying that it was a mystery to him how this man could
have lived as long as he did.*

   *Mario Battani, friend and colleague of Rodestrom,
head of the Institute for Ultra Low Temperature Physics
in Cerveteri, near Rome, had come to London at the
request of the authorities and insisted, 'I have no reason
not to believe that my friend Bengt is on the island of
Samso and in the best of health. The fact is, the dead man
could really have been a younger brother of Rodestrom,
but he was a crackpot who liked to think he was
important.' The authorities are up against a mystery.
The similarity with the 'Torre-Double' case which took
place two years ago, the identity of which remains
unclarified, is striking.*

'They could easily clarify the identity by comparing
fingerprints,' I said and shoved the newspaper back.

'There are probably no fingerprints of Torre. And he
hasn't been found to this day.'

'But in the Rodestrom case . . . '

Andrew shrugged his shoulders. 'Perhaps he
refused.'

'Why would he have refused?'

'I don't know.' He wiped the crumbs together and put
them onto an empty plate.

'One thing is very peculiar, though. Both Torre and
Rodestrom belonged to Roughtrade's MIDAS crew, at
least at the beginning.'

'Do you think there's any connection?'

'Buchan, head of NASA Secret Service, asked me
some very strange questions before we left for Nanguneri. They didn't make any sense to me. Nothing
concrete, mind you, he probably just wanted to sound
me out. "Kenneth," I said to him, "I've been in orbit for
the past six months. I have no idea what you're talking
about. You'll have to tell me what you want to know."
He said that he needed certain information because of

the Torre kidnapping. They had come across some strange facts that could possibly have something to do with MIDAS.' He leaned back and looked at me. 'Peter, do you believe in the resurrection of the flesh?'

'Are you asking me as a Christian or as a technician?'

'I'm asking you, Peter.' He studied my face carefully, his dark eyes full of life. A bit of egg had established itself in his moustache. I would have loved to have flicked it away with my finger, but refrained from doing so.

'If you mean cloning . . . '

Andrew dismissed the thought contemptuously. 'It's child's play and besides, it takes too much time.'

A cabin steward arrived and cleared the remains of our breakfast away. His movements were so slow it was fascinating to watch him. His hands, almost black, were unbelievably small and delicate.

'If I hadn't been present at his death, I could easily believe Roughtrade's still living and carrying on the project. Only Roughtrade could, you know.' He was silent for a moment, then he said, 'In order to finance it, he'd use slave-trade. Just like the bastard!'

'Slave-trade. How could anyone today . . . ?'

'We're landing,' Andrew interrupted and pointed out of the window. The tops of palm trees were in sight. The Sultan Ahmet had reached its destination at Katunayake near Negombo, the international airport of Colombo.

5

The Realm of the Sinhalas

'Would you like some tea?' the inspector asked, lavishly scooping sugar into the three cups and slowly filling them with milk.

'Yes, please,' I said and Andrew nodded.

Steaming black tea was poured and it changed to a pleasant light brown colour. The inspector passed the cups over his desk. He glanced directly at us and it was only then that we realized that his eyes were a bright blue, unusual for someone with his dark skin.

'Are you a physicist, Mr Baldenham?'

'No, I'm a mathematician.'

'And you, Mr Kirk, are you a mathematician, too?'

'No, I'm a telemetry engineer.'

'Just what does a telemetry engineer do?'

'He checks the alignment of laser mirrors and antennas in order to establish communication links between satellites and ground stations as well as between satellites.'

'Very interesting. Did you ever work for SDI?'

'No, I only worked on the EFOS project. Never had anything to do with weapons in space.'

'You wouldn't be here obviously if you had, would you, Mr Kirk?'

'I guess so, sir.'

The inspector must have noticed that I was growing

very cross as he suddenly flashed one of his most charming smiles.

'Please don't interpret this as a cross-examination, but I'm responsible for security matters in this country and the times are very unsafe. Whites are no longer welcome in countries of the Third World, and Americans least of all. We've got to keep an eye on you. There could be some trouble. I hope you understand my position.

'And about this piece of equipment that was found on your person, Mr Kirk? Just what is it?'

'It's an EMPU, an Electronic Magnetic Pulse Unit, in other words, an eraser.'

'Isn't it also called an electronic brass knuckles?'

'Some people call it that.'

'And it's used to destroy electronic equipment?'

'Not to destroy it, sir. In case of emergency, artificial electro-magnetic impulses can erase specific contents of a definite memory area or stop a faulty program. An astronaut always carries his eraser with him. When a skylab is constructed, dozens of components are in motion. These are manoeuvred into place by computer-controlled haulers. In case of emergency, an astronaut, who moves in the construction area, has to be able to intervene within a matter of seconds in order to erase the faulty program and activate the correct one.'

'Certainly, your brass knuckles are only necessary in outer space, aren't they?'

'An astronaut always carries his eraser. It's a sign of his profession.'

'Theoretically, however, one could also interfere with the board electronics of a plane, the data memory of a bank or telephone installations, or . . . ah . . . even stop a pacemaker.'

'That's right, sir, as long as hardware is not involved.'

'I call that a dangerous toy, Mr Kirk.'

'No astronaut would ever play with it and misuse by an unauthorized person is not possible as the sensor on the wrist band comes equipped with a secret code. I alone know the code and only I can activate the eraser with it.'

'Yes, I know, Mr Kirk.' He took my passport and leafed through it, undecided.

'As you do not have a work permit for this country, you won't need this fabulous instrument.'

'I don't like to part with my personal belongings, especially something so important to me.'

'That's life, Mr Kirk.' The inspector took a dark brown jiffy bag from his desk and my brass knuckles fell into it with a soft thud. He sealed it with a fast-drying plastic and handed me the control stub after tearing it off from the edge of the bag and stamping it.

'Your toy will be returned to you on departure from this country. Have you got some brass knuckles, too, Mr Baldenham?'

'No, I'm not an astronaut.'

'But you've worked in outer space, haven't you?'

'No, I've never been in outer space.'

'And the sign of your profession is a calculator?'

'Wrong!' Andrew tapped his sun-burned brow. 'My head, and I'm certainly not going to leave it here for you!'

The inspector broke out into a loud guffaw, which sounded surprisingly deep and hollow for someone of his slight stature. It was as if someone had set a compressor into operation inside his chest.

We both looked at him somewhat startled until he was able to control himself again.

'Where are you going to stay?'

I shrugged my shoulders.

'I recommend the Taprobane. It's just been renovated.'

'We would like to leave as soon as possible for Trincomalee,' Andrew said.

'It's the rainy season on the east coast at the moment.'

'That's exactly what we're looking forward to.'

'Then I wish you a pleasant stay.' He handed us our passports from behind his desk. 'Should you encounter any difficulties on your journey, just phone and have yourself put through to Inspector Kirtisinghe. I'm very well-known here.'

On the way to Colombo we passed a great many houses that had been ravaged and burnt out. Some of them could have been from the Tamil Wars, others were more recent. The former tourist hotels along the Negombo and Wattala Beach were closed off with barbed wire entanglement. Refugees from Thailand had taken over the hotels, swarming in hordes. Shortly after passing through the village of Wattala, we were caught in a crowd of people. Our driver tried to back up, but in the meantime, buses and rickshaws had congested the street behind us and he couldn't move. People in tattered clothes, most of them barefoot, ran shouting across the street and shook their fists in protest. Their anger was directed at an overloaded army truck. A young man had climbed up on top of it and slashed the tarpaulin. They tried to drag sacks full of rice to the edge of the truck and throw them down, but soldiers with clubs were soon at hand to prevent them.

Our taxi driver leaned back in resignation and, with a sigh, lit a cigarette. 'People wery hungry. Thai people much foods from UNO; our people nothing eat. Moslems no work, wery poor. Bad military government.'

Suddenly shots rang out. He ducked behind the steering wheel. The people scattered in all directions, shrieking in panic, while the overloaded truck continued on its way. Rice cascaded from its sides. Emaciated hands hastily scraped the grains up from the asphalt in spite of the busy traffic. A young man sat on the curb, dazed and with his face covered in blood, while another tried to help him.

'Bad,' our driver said. 'Bad,' he repeated as if to emphasize his point.

'The room costs $300 a night. They're crazy!'

'Listen, Pete!' Andrew called from under the shower, where he was soaping himself down. 'You can get a room for $300 or one for $1, there's nothing in between. Why should I give up what every elephant has a right to.'

'What does an elephant have a right to?'

'A bath a day.'

'Are you ready?'

'No, it'll take me awhile yet.'

I sat on the bed and counted my cash. It was appalling how little we had left!

'It doesn't look good at all,' I said to Andrew when he finally appeared with a towel wrapped around his head.

'Yeah, we ought to have one of those Roughtrade machines all right.'

'What's a Roughtrade machine?'

'Don't you know the story of Rumpelstiltskin? Someone has a spinning wheel and with it straw can be turned into gold. With the Roughtrade machine, you put in a Singapore dollar and – ring-a-ling – it'll start spitting out Singapore dollars. Magic Table! Gold Donkey! Club in the Sack!'

'All that could only happen in fairy tales.'

'Yes,' he answered, lost in thought, sitting down cross-legged on the carpet like a fakir, 'in fairy tales . . . !'

As we stepped out of the hotel, we were accosted by a

horde of emaciated figures – beggars, self-appointed travel guides, rickshaw drivers. They saw in us the only bright spot in their day. A policeman pulled out his gun and threatened them back, directing us brusquely into one of the waiting taxis. It was a ramshackle old black Peugeot which must have come off the assembly line long before my time. The driver, a slight, very young man in jeans and a sports shirt, spoke excellent English.

'Cambridge Institute,' he said proudly. 'And three years as a foreign worker in Bahrain.'

'How old are you?' I asked.

'Twenty-eight.' He didn't look a day older than seventeen. 'Would you like to go on a sightseeing tour of the island?'

'With your car?'

'Oh, it's in good condition. It might belong to the cooperative, but I take care of it myself.'

I looked inquiringly at Andrew. He nodded.

'Be at the hotel by eight o'clock tomorrow morning.'

'Okay.'

The Taprobane was just behind the Senate on the corner of Church and York Street right near the harbour. From the Harbour Room on the roof of the building, there was a splendid view over the passenger jetty, the Queen Elizabeth Quay and other port facilities. We were just on the point of taking the elevator up when the lights went out.

'Please remain in the lobby,' the porter announced to the guests who had assembled, mostly bored tea and spice tradesmen, 'we're having an air raid warning!'

Boys carried in clay bowls full of oil with burning wicks swimming in them and put them on the tables. A soft, flickering light filled the hall. Then the gong sounded and called us to dinner. Ghost-like figures appeared to banquet in the dining room. I strained my ears, waiting anxiously for the roar of planes or bombs exploding, but the night air was only filled with the honking of cars and the ringing of rickshaw bells. I was, in fact, rather disappointed when the lights flared up again. The manager appeared at the reception, his hands spread out. Bowing over like a circus director, he proclaimed. 'We've just received the "all-clear" signal. The blackout is over.'

'What did breakfast cost?'
  'Thirty dollars.'
  'For the two of us?'
  'No, thirty each.'
  'And for the spooky candlelight dinner yesterday evening?'
  'Eighty dollars.'
  'For the two of us?'
  'No, eighty each.'
  'Jesus! They've gone mad. It can't go on like this, Andrew!'
  'From now on we'll have to get our own food and fend for ourselves.'
  The driver studied us in his rear-view mirror. 'I'll try to get something for you, but it won't be easy.'
  'Surely they'll sell us a few bananas and coconuts.'
  'Perhaps,' he said. 'But they don't have much themselves. They have to hand over everything to the cooperative. And they're afraid of being punished for profiteering if they sell anything on the black market.'
  'For real money?' The moment I opened my mouth I knew that I ought not to have said it. He laughed sarcastically.
  'These people are not allowed to take any foreign currency. Only the big hotels, and they have a hundred per cent mark up. I'll see what I can do for you. By the way, it'll take at least ten hours to Trincomalee.'
  'Who told you we wanted to go to Trincomalee?' Andrew asked suspiciously and leaned forward.

'All the sightseeing tours start with Anuradhapura, Trincomalee, Sigiriya, Polonnaruwa . . . '

'That's not true!' Andrew interrupted him. 'Take the road to Kandy and from there to Batticaloa!'

'Okay, okay!' The driver shrugged his shoulders. 'I'll take you wherever you like.'

6

The Column of Fire

Late that afternoon we arrived in Kandy. On the artificial
lake in front of the Temple of the Tooth, waterlilies were
almost in bloom. The buds were still closed, looming
like purple-coloured arrowheads out of the water. On
the shore, some rickshaw drivers were idly waiting for
customers. Their silhouettes stood out like paper cut-
outs against the glistening surface of the lake. Three
monks were resting on a balustrade under a saffron-
coloured sunshade, sleepy and fat like castrated tom-
cats. Their faces were void of expression. We didn't
stop, continuing our journey up into the mountains in
the direction of Maha Oya. The road got worse and the
Peugeot rattled and clattered. Clouds of dust drifted
into the car.

'Let's stop for a rest soon,' the driver said, and spat
out of the window.

He stopped just before we came to a bridge. Its rusty
arches stretched over an almost dried-out riverbed. The
driver got out, went around the car and took our bags
out of the trunk.

'Hey, what're you doing?' Andrew asked.

'Please wait here for me. I shall try to get some gas for
the car and something to eat. I'll be back in half an
hour.'

We got out and took our bags. Andrew leaned over

the rail of the bridge. 'This must be the Muhaweli Ganga. If it is, we're almost halfway there.'

Three giant trees were standing on an island in the riverbed. They seemed to be dying. Whole clusters of long leathery fruit hung from their bare grey boughs.

'What are they?' I asked in surprise.

'A type of bat found in this region. They're called flying foxes. They sleep during the daytime and hunt at night.'

About one hundred yards from the bridge, the riverbed formed a deep hole. Women were crouching on the shore and washing. In the eerie stillness, the slapping sound of the clothes on the stones, the voices and laughter seemed unusually loud.

We turned around. Suddenly, out of nowhere, a teenage girl and a young boy appeared in front of us. The girl, perhaps twelve or thirteen years old, wore a tattered dress made of faded blue cotton. Her small breasts could be seen through the tatters. The little boy was three or four years old. His head had been shorn and his snotty nose was running. His only piece of clothing was a short shirt, which didn't even cover his penis that he was fumbling with in his excitement. He looked at us innocently. She was very hostile. She brushed the tangled black hair from her forehead and opened a dirty bundle that she was carrying in her hand. She pulled out a flying fox. The small, grey, furry face reflected a pitiable mixture of drowsiness and terror. The long body with its naked, wrinkled, dark grey flying membranes quivered helplessly in the girl's clutch.

'Hey!' She said arrogantly. 'Ten dollars – kill!' She squeezed the tiny throat of the bat-like creature with her thumb and forefinger. 'Eat! Ten dollars! Kill! Eat!' She raised her chin impatiently in demand.

'These animals are protected under the wild-life

conservation law.' Andrew tried to explain to her. 'Don't kill! Forbidden!'

'Ten dollars! Kill! Eat!'

The mouth of the creature opened to let out an inaudible scream. The small blue-grey lips bared to reveal sharp, wizened teeth.

'Forbidden! Do you understand?' Andrew screamed at her. She spat on the ground in a savage rage and with dancing steps approached me.

'Ten dollars!' she demanded. I shook my head. She slugged the creature angrily into the bundle and hurled a few incomprehensible curses at us.

'Ten dollars, Mister! Fuck! Make fuck!' She pulled her cotton dress up to uncover her naked, hairless cunt. She opened her legs and began to sway her hips in a circular movement.

'Make fuck, Mister! Ten dollars!'

'Fuck!' the young boy repeated, in all innocence.

Suddenly, she stopped swaying her hips and urinated in front of me. I was so surprised that I could only stare at the yellow puddle growing larger in front of me. Then she darted off, shrieking, and the young boy followed with a howl of triumph.

When he saw my face, Andrew couldn't contain his laughter. 'That's the aftermath of mass tourism, Pete.'

Stones flew from the bushes on the other side of the street. Fortunately, they missed their mark.

'Beat it,' Andrew shouted, 'or I'll give you a sound thrashing on your little ass!'

A flock of black birds were startled into flight and began to circle above us, noiselessly.

Upstream, a woman called. Perhaps a name.

The driver brought us a huge helping of rice with curry wrapped in a banana leaf, two papayas, half a dozen bananas and three coconuts.

'I was only able to get one helping of rice,' he said, opening the coconuts with a large rusty knife.

'Help yourself!' I invited him to join us. 'There's enough for the three of us.'

'I've already eaten,' he assured us. I didn't believe him, but said nothing. I ate the meal with relish. The coconut milk was cool and soothed the sharp flavour of the curry. 'What did you pay for all this?'

'About forty rupees.'

I began to calculate. 'That's no more than a dollar and a half.'

'That's a day's wages here.'

'You mean our breakfast in Taprobane cost us a month's salary?'

He nodded and sipped some milk from his coconut. 'On the other hand, I paid two thousand rupees for gas for the car. Eighty dollars.'

'That means that a tank of gasoline costs a normal worker . . . '

' . . . more than two months' wages. That's right, sir.'

Andrew sniggered. 'Hasn't changed a bit, Pete. Exactly the same story thirty years ago.'

'Then there's something wrong!'

'People here have been asking themselves for a long time how a white man could spend as much in a day as they earn in a year.'

'I've seen officers spend more in one evening than a rubber tapster earns in a lifetime,' our driver said, and threw his coconut carelessly on the road. It rolled over the asphalt with a hollow thud and I automatically thought of a head rolling from the blade of a guillotine.

Late in the afternoon, we reached the lowlands. Water holes could be seen glistening in the distance. Grey water buffaloes with mighty black horns lay wallowing in the mire, their hides gleaming with mud.

'The first time I was here, this whole area was

flooded,' Andrew said. 'A typhoon. The ocean had surged forward more than forty miles inland. For days on end, survivors were picked up from the palm trees with a helicopter. Thousands were drowned. All the hotels on the coast disappeared. Everything was washed away. There'd never been anything like it before. They broke through the coral reef along the coast in order to get chalk and the water coursed through. That was a rude awakening.'

We drove past a large military installation which was protected by an electric fence and barbed wire. Heavy duty trucks were lined up in a row, one beside the other. Their tarpaulins were covered with dust. In the distance, on the airfield, an ancient Phantom flew in the direction of the ocean. It made a sharp turn westwards and screeched over us in the direction of the mountains.

On our right, the lagoon of Batticaloa glistened and on our left, the ocean frothed over spacious sandy beaches. To the east, the clouds were towering high.

We sat on the terrace of the Batticaloa Hotel and were obviously the only overnight guests. Two officers were sitting at a far-off table drinking Glenfiddich whisky. Our driver had gone on to the next village to find cheaper accommodation for himself.

A sullen waiter brought our beer and set it down in front of us without saying a word. The manager, on the other hand, was much more eager to please. He was a plump, friendly man. His black hair was greased down with pomade and brushed back over his head and his moustache, which had been cut with exact precision, was perched just above his upper lip.

'All the other hotels are closed down at this time of year. You'll have the beach to yourselves.' He cast a searching glance at the sky.

The waiter brought a bottle of Glenfiddich, two glasses and a bucket full of ice.

'We didn't order that,' I said.

'The two gentlemen would like you to be their guests,' the manager replied, and nodded with his head to the officers.

'But I don't want any . . . ' Andrew patted me on the arm and shook his head unobtrusively.

Both officers bowed their heads in our direction and raised their glasses.

'You know how I detest this pack of smart-assed officers,' I hissed.

'Yes, I know, but be quiet!'

'Why?'

'Because the military has the real power in this country. They rule over life and death all over the world. Believe me, that's a fact of life that'll never change, even in the so-called democracies.'

We had not had any whisky for months and my aversion to the military quickly disappeared, especially when they both picked up their canes from the table and left the terrace.

'This bay was once famous for its singing fish. At full moon, you could hear them singing in the lagoon,' Andrew said. 'But the sewage from the hotels soon put an end to that.'

The ocean swept over the beach and thundered over the coral reef out in the bay. A warm, humid breeze blew in from the ocean. We watched a fisherman stomping knee-deep in water across the bay. He was holding a pair of rush-woven oyster baskets over his shoulder and had wrapped his vest around himself like a loincloth. He stopped again and again and looked up at the menacing dark sky.

Andrew grabbed my arm. 'There it is again!' He pointed upwards.

The eastern horizon was almost dark, veiled in a dense sea of blue-black clouds. In the foreground, the heavy surf flared white against the reef. Then, high above the tops of the palm trees, a strange cloud formation rose, glowing at first pale salmon, then blazing red and finally a deep blood red. It must have reached into the upper atmosphere as the sun had long since set behind the mountains. It looked like a mushroom cloud after an atomic bomb explosion. Then, the phenomenon disappeared, dissolving itself in a matter of minutes like a whirlwind from the bottom upwards. However, it left me with an ominous feeling which seemed to spread over the whole coastline.

'What was that?' I asked.

'I don't know. Perhaps a local meteorological phenomenon, the eye of a hurricane that lacks the power to develop. It happened the first time just before the flood disaster and it keeps reappearing again and again. The fisherman fear it as a bad omen.'

'Do you believe in such things?' I asked.

He was silent for a long time and I thought he didn't want to answer. However, then he looked at me and said, 'Yes, I believe in such things.'

The fisherman vanished in the darkness.

The manager personally served us a delicious fish dish in a spicy, sweet peanut butter sauce with rice and chopped vegetables.

'What brought you to Asia, Andrew?'

'I was searching for a method of meditation similar to the flushing principle – a method that would flush all troubles and sorrow out of the cerebral cortex while the great revelation of higher mathematics would appear inside my brain.'

'Did you find what you were looking for?'

He snorted contemptuously, 'What I found were bumbling, babbling idiots, who were convinced that they alone had a lease on karma and that abolishing all intellectual reasoning was in itself an ordination into mysticism. Nothing but hippies who hate the system.'

He looked out to sea. Darkness had fallen and the surf

flared up against the reef. 'Nevertheless, I learned a lot from them, Pete,' he continued. 'The Orient is a giant, colourful storybook full of splendid tales, but the reality behind all the pomp is filth, misery, drudgery and cruelty – as in all slave-trading societies in the days of old or today, whether in the east or west.' He swirled his empty glass around in his hand. 'It's a shame. We could have changed all that.'

'How?'

He shrugged his shoulders and didn't answer.

I can't remember exactly what we talked about on that particular evening, but the whisky bottle was gradually emptied. It started to rain – a pleasant, pattering, warm rain. We couldn't find our bungalows at first. They were tiny, simple huts at the other end of the hotel grounds.

'Why, in the name of heaven, did they have to give us the last two huts!' Andrew cursed, splashing through the puddles. 'They're all empty anyway!'

Five minutes later, I was sound asleep.

I heard an explosion and when I looked up, I saw a column of fire bursting out of the sea. It rose higher and higher into the sky with a thundering noise, rotating like a blazing top. A roar filled the air, and then excited cries. The fisherman stood in the shallow water and pointed upwards. Someone was hammering on the door and calling my name. The whole sky was ablaze and the roar of the column of fire grew more intense. A soldier appeared at my window. He brushed the screen aside and broke the glass with strokes of his rifle butt.

'Out of here, mister! Quickly! You've got to get out of here!'

I got up in a daze, grabbed my clothes and stuffed them into my bag.

'Quickly, Mister! This way!'

'What's the matter?'

'The house is on fire!'

I climbed out of the window. It was already light. The air was full of smoke and the glare of fire. There were sparks in the air. The sun was rising above the coral reef. Soldiers were running around in confusion. One of them was fidgeting with a small fire-extinguisher which wouldn't work.

'Andrew!' I screamed when I realized his hut was up in flames. The roof had already caved in and the blaze of the dried reeds on the thatched roof caused the crowd to shrink back in horror. The wind drove the flames further inland. The first flames started to lick the thatched roof of my hut. Finally, the fire extinguisher started working. White foam spattered over the wooden wall of the hut and flooded the roof.

'Where is the man?' I screamed.

One of the soldiers pointed in the direction of the main building.

'Has he been injured?'

I couldn't understand him because a helicopter with flashing navigation lights was hovering directly above us, getting ready to land. The pressure of the air from his propellers forced the smoke downwards, so that I couldn't see. I turned away coughing. Suddenly, the manager was standing in front of me. I didn't recognise him at first, because he was wearing one of those colourful, native, wrap-around cloths, and the upper part of his body was naked. It was only then that I realized that all I had on was my underpants.

'I am so very sorry, Mr Kirk,' he lamented.

'Where is he? Has anything happened to him?' I slipped into my jeans.

'His feet. A roof beam crashed down on him. They've taken him up front. A doctor from the military base is with him.'

'**Why didn't someone wake me sooner?**'

'I tried, Mr Kirk, but I couldn't wake you and the door was locked.'

I fished my clothes out of my bag and slipped them on, shoving my shirt into my jeans. As I ran along the winding path past the tiny huts with their flower-beds, I slipped and landed in a bed of mimosa which covered the ground like a hard, tough carpet. At that very moment, the mimosa closed their petals. Cursing, I struggled to my feet and continued running. On the parking lot in front of the hotel, a helicopter with its propellers turning was ready for take-off. When I arrived, two soldiers were heaving a stretcher onto it. Blood plasma swung from a support.

'Andrew!' I roared in order to be heard above the noise of the chopper. The figure on the stretcher did not respond. 'Andrew!' He was unconscious. A man in a white coat appeared at the entrance. I ran up to him, but a soldier with a submachine gun barred the way. 'Take me with you, doctor!' The doctor didn't answer, but held his arm up to ward me off. 'Please, listen to me, doctor! I'm his friend!' I tried to push my way past the soldier, but he cocked his rifle and pointed it at me.

'No!' He shouted.

'He's my friend! Don't you understand? Please let me see him!'

'No!' the soldier stamped his foot and glared at me in anger. He was serious. I let my hands fall in resignation and helpless rage. I had to stand by and watch while the helicopter started and took off further inland.

'Asshole!' I said to the soldier, but he obviously didn't understand me. I turned around. The sun had risen. The soldiers had the fire under control. The manager hastened towards me, wringing his hands.

'How did the fire start! Did Mr Baldenham smoke in bed?'

'Mr Baldenham is a non-smoker. Where've they taken him?'

'To the military hospital in Colombo, I think. His legs look real bad. A beam fell on them, do you understand. He'll have to be operated on.'

'Didn't he leave a message for me?'

'Sorry, Mr Kirk, no. He was . . . how do you say . . . unconscious. The doctor said he'd have to be operated on right away. Don't worry, Mr Kirk! He's getting the best treatment. Everything possible will be done for him. I'll have them make you your breakfast.'

'I would like to place a phone call to Negombo – Inspector Kirtinsinghe.'

'Have you got the number?'

'No, damn it all, you'll have to ask the operator! He must be with the police or the secret service.'

When the manager returned he had changed into European clothes which were, as always, immaculate. His hair was pomaded and had a pleasant, attar of roses scent. A waiter had set up an opulent breakfast. Egghoppers, warm, small round pancakes made of rice meal with a fried egg in it, fresh papayas, small honey-sweet bananas, toast, marmalade, butter and a pot of tea. I couldn't eat anything at all – not a bite. I had a dreadful headache and was still numb from shock.

'They don't know of any Inspector Kirtisinghe at the police headquarters in Negombo.'

'That's absolutely impossible! He told me personally that he is very well-known.'

The manager shrugged his shoulders. 'I don't know him.'

'Can I speak to the doctor who took care of him when it happened?'

'He was flown to Colombo with him.'

'Then put a call through to the military hospital.'

'They won't be able to give you any information on the phone, Mr Kirk.'

'Couldn't you get one of those high-ranking officers

from the base to put in a good word for us. Perhaps the two officers who offered us the whisky yesterday. You must know them well enough to ask.'

He shrugged his shoulders, obviously ill at ease. 'I don't know them well enough to ask them to do me any favours, Mr Kirk.'

'I don't understand.'

'It would be best if you drive back to Colombo and get in touch with Inspector Kirtisinghe personally. Perhaps he can get you the permission to visit your friend in hospital, Mr Kirk. I'll inform your driver. No need to pay for your stay here – you've experienced enough unpleasantness as is. Oh! You haven't even touched your breakfast, Mr Kirk. What a shame! Never mind, I'll have a lunch packed for your journey.'

He obviously wanted to get rid of me without any more trouble. And he was afraid of the military who frequented his hotel. But why?

I was very silent and depressed on the journey back to Colombo. At noon, we stopped for a rest in the mountains. An elephant was loading a truck with logs that half a dozen other elephants had hauled up from the almost inaccessible valley of the jungle below. No command was given. The perfect team work between driver and elephant was amazing. The drover wrapped a heavy chain around the end of the log to which a picket had been attached; the leading elephant, whose hide on its trunk and forehead was chafed from the work, packed the chain with its trunk and raised one end of the log – ten men couldn't have moved it – to the loading space on the waiting truck. While the driver released the chain and attached it to the next log, the elephant trotted to the other end of the first log and shoved it with its forehead onto the truck.

My driver looked at his watch and studied the position of the sun.

'Watch!' he said.

The elephant had just heaved the upper part of an even larger log on to the loading space and, instead of trotting to the other end to finish the job, turned to the driver and curved its trunk. The driver stepped onto the bend and, with an elegant movement, was carried upwards until he was sitting on the neck of the animal behind its huge ears. Then the elephant made its way downhill into the jungle.

'Does it stop right in the middle of its work?'

'No one in this world could persuade an elephant to work a second longer when the sun is at its zenith. Six hours – from daybreak to noon – and that since working elephants have existed.'

'And what do they do the rest of the day?'

'They go for a swim and look for food in the jungle.'

A bath a day – even an elephant had the right to one, Andrew had said.

'Let's get going!' I said impatiently. I had to find out what had happened to Andrew. I couldn't get rid of an overwhelming feeling of dread.

'Have you a family?' I asked to divert my thoughts to another subject.

'I had a wife,' he said, 'but it's a sad story. You have enough troubles as it is, I won't bore you.'

'Oh, please tell me!'

'My wife and I had both studied English at the Cambridge Institute and qualified for a job in a foreign country. We both found work in Bahrain. They prefer couples. It saves them a lot of trouble, you know.'

A heavy rain had started to fall. The windscreen wipers could hardly keep the screen clean.

'Have you ever seen such a contract, Sir? As long as you are healthy and can work, everything is all right. But when you're ill, you're out of luck. And it's even worse if you need a doctor. That's what happened to me. I had an accident on the building site and had to spend four months in hospital. The money I had earned was not enough to pay the hospital bills and my wife's small savings were soon used up. Then, they started holding her wages back. I was told they'd taken her into "preventative custody" – a labour camp – so that she wouldn't be able to leave the country before the hospital costs were paid. A few weeks later, I was informed that she had died of typhus. It was only when I was home again that I learned from one of her colleagues that she had been put into a brothel. She committed suicide there. No one could tell me what they did with her body. Perhaps they buried her in a hurry or threw her into the sea. After all, she was only a foreigner – an unbeliever in their eyes – and a whore on top of that. I told you it wasn't a beautiful story, didn't I, Sir?'

'You're right, a horrible story.'

We drove on in silence for a while.

'Are you working for EFOS?'

'How do you know that?'

'From the manager of the Batticaola.'

'And where did he get the information?'

He shrugged his shoulders. 'No idea. You know,' he said after a moment, 'to be quite frank with you, I don't like Americans, but EFOS is a thorn in the flesh of the oil sheikhs. It serves them right. More and more countries are now joining the International Energy Commission and the sheikhs can stuff their barrels of oil up their asses. They'd like nothing better than to shoot your Sunbirds down from the sky.'

'It wouldn't be all that easy.' I said. 'They are pretty high, you know!'

'Shall I drive you to Negombo and wait for you there?' he asked.

'Yes, that would be very kind of you.'

Somehow or other I suspected that Inspector Kirti-singhe wouldn't be there.

'He's on a business trip,' a dark-skinned young man explained. He was sitting at Inspector Kirtisinghe's desk and eyed me through his thick glasses. They made his dark pupils seem overly large. 'Can I help you?'

I told him about the fire and explained that I would like to visit my injured friend.

'I shall make inquiries. Wait outside, please.'

Through the window on the other side of the corridor, I had an excellent view of the international airport of Katunayake. Thirty years ago, according to Andrew, sixty to eighty planes had taken off and landed in a single day. Now, PanAm, British Airways, Quantas and Singapore Airlines were exclusively permitted to land and, at that, with weekly flights only. The burnt-out wreck of a Lufthansa Jumbo jet, blown up by some terrorists, lay on the other side of the landing strip like the gutted body of a giant shellfish. The incident had happened ten years ago, but no one had found it necessary to clear away the remains. The airport lay deserted. The red reflection of the setting sun could be seen in the tower windows.

'Mr Kirk,' a quiet voice called behind me. I turned around. It was the officer. I had not heard the door open. He had taken his glasses off and squinted up at me near-sightedly. 'I've got some sad news for you, Mr Kirk. Mr Baldenham died this afternoon.'

'*What*?' I had to hold on to the wall for support as my legs were threatening to collapse under me. 'Oh God, it can't be!'

'Yes, unfortunately.' He shoved his glasses back onto his nose and looked over my shoulder out of the window. 'Did you know him well?'

'He was my friend.'

He nodded. 'Then I must request you to drive with me to Colombo in order to identify the body. It's just a formality, you understand.'

'I'll have to get my bag and pay the driver!'

'Please do. In the meantime, I'll order one of our police cars.'

He had been taken to a cold-storage chamber in the basement of the police headquarters. More than a dozen corpses lay in black plastic bags or under sheets on stretchers on wheels. An official pulled back the sheet. They had bandaged up his jawbone as rigor mortis had not yet set in. This made him look rather annoyed. I realized that his lower legs were gone because where they should have been, there was nothing. The sheet lay flat on the table. I asked him to fold back the sheet completely. Strangely enough, at that moment, it was this multilation that shocked me more that his unexpected death. Both legs had been amputated just above the ankles. The wounds had been hastily sewn together and were still encrusted with blood. Otherwise, his body had not been hurt at all. A yellow elastic band with a labeled card hung from his right wrist. When I saw him lying there naked before me, a helpless and mournful sight, I had to fight back the tears.

'What did he die of?'

The official glanced at the card and let the elastic band snap back. 'Heart failure during the operation according to what the doctor has written here.'

'What happens to him now?'

'The body hasn't been released yet. Perhaps someone will want to have an autopsy performed. His urn will be sent to his relatives. Do you know them?'

'I don't believe he has any. He never mentioned anyone.'

'May I hand his personal belongings over to you, then?'

'Of course.'

I followed him into an office with rows of lockers. An older official with curly white hair and an enormous walrus moustache piled his belongings onto the table:

his shoes, his pants, a worn leather jacket, his shirts and underwear, socks, towels, his toilet case, his notebook and writing utensils, his wallet, passport and money. There was nothing missing as far as I could see. He checked every article individually on the list and then handed the list to me for my signature before packing the things into Andrew's bag.

It was already dark when I finally left the headquarters and stepped out onto the street. Motorbike rickshaws putt-putted by, bicycle rickshaws rang their bells. Pedlars were spreading their wares out on the pavements.

I was still dazed. Trying to find my way on foot to the Taprobane, I suddenly stopped dead in my tracks. How on earth had it been possible to save all his personal belongings from the burning bungalow cabin if they had pulled Andrew out from under a fallen beam at the very last moment?

The following day was Christmas – the saddest Christmas ever. The PanAm office was closed for two days. A small, plastic Christmas tree covered with angel's hair and tiny, coloured, gaudy lights had been set up in the lobby of the Taprobane Hotel. In the lift, *Jinglebells* and *Holy Night* droned softly. The weather was sultry and stiflingly hot. The ocean lay like molten silver under a misty white sky. There was no breeze. I stayed in the coolness of my air-conditioned room and racked my brains about what had happened that night in Batticaloa. The longer I thought about it, the more incredible it all seemed. A small wooden hut with a thatched roof would have gone up in flames in a matter of seconds. And yet, soldiers from the military base had arrived fully equipped in the middle of the night. A doctor was there in no time at all, a helicopter and pilot were ready for take-off. But why Andrew? What did they want from him? Why had they mutilated and then killed him?

I didn't trust the military – I mistrust the military on principle. They rule over life and death, Andrew had said. How right he was! But what would such people want with Andrew? An act of revenge? Why Andrew? He had never harmed anyone in his life. People had always taken advantage of him because he was too kind. The more I thought, the less sense it all made. In fact, it made no sense at all.

Two days later, a Monday, when I stepped out of the PanAm office on the Jayatilleka Mawatha Boulevard, the air seemed even more stifling than ever. The smell of rottenness and human excrement was overwhelming. To the north, above the harbour, thunderclouds rose high as they did every afternoon, only to dissolve completely by sundown – a weak promise of refreshing rain.

I leafed through the ticket once again and slid it into my pocket. The plane was arriving from Sidney via Singapore and would be leaving at eight o'clock in the morning. In fifteen hours, I would be out of this inferno.

'Mr Kirk,' I heard a familiar voice behind me. A black car stopped at the curb. The driver who had taken us to Batticaloa was sitting in it. He was wearing a rumpled, light grey suit, which made him look even thinner, and a large, dark pair of sunglasses. His face almost disappeared behind them. 'Please take a seat!' He bent over and opened the car door. I got in and sat up in front beside him.

He seemed very nervous and when he lit a cigarette, I noticed that his hands were trembling.

'What's the matter?' I asked.

'I've got something to tell you,' he said, steering the car through the chaotic traffic. 'Have you got a moment?'

'Yes. But I'm flying to New York tomorrow morning. There's no reason for me to stay here anymore.'

He nodded. We had just passed Prince Park. He drove into a quiet side street and parked at the back entrance to a restaurant in Wolfendahl Street.

'I'm sure you've heard of Nancy Tanner,' he said.

'The actress?'

'Yes.'

I told him that I'd seen several of her films on video and asked him why he wanted to know.

He hesitated at first, but then told me the most incredible story. He claimed that he had witnessed the shooting of Nancy Tanner. According to him, an officer had shot her to death at the back entrance of a club. The next day he had seen her again, alive and healthy, in broad daylight on the Janadhipathi Mawatha Boulevard. I told him that I couldn't really believe his story. Then he said something very strange.

'I'm a devout Buddhist, Mr Kirk. I believe in rebirth, but whatever this is, it's something unnatural, something wicked and evil.'

Hadn't Andrew mentioned something about rebirth? No, he had asked: *Do you believe in the resurrection of the flesh*? What could he have meant by that?

'I know exactly when it happened,' he said.

'When what happened?'

'How she fell into their hands. It was perhaps a month ago. She was here in Colombo. She was staying at the Taprobane just like you, Mr Kirk. I drove her from the Vihara Devi Park to the Hotel. She was very nervous. The next day she was hospitalised. She allegedly took an overdose of cocaine and they even found cocaine on her. Miss Tanner likes to drink a glass of champagne now and again, but she would never take hard drugs. I know these people! It was all a swindle – the charges against her, her indictment, her deportation to the USA.' He took off his sunglasses and looked me straight in the eye.

'Mr Kirk, I'd like to tell you something I've never told

anyone else before. When she was here a month ago, Miss Tanner gave me a letter for her manager, a Mr Fred Kissinger.'

'The film director?'

'I think he was a film director. However, later, after she'd become a famous star, he decided to take over as her manager. She had a meeting arranged with him here in Colombo, but he didn't keep the appointment. "Mr Kissinger will arrive in a few days time and will be staying at the Taprobane," she said. "Would you be kind enough to give him this letter in person. I can't wait for him any longer." I replied, "Of course, I'll be glad to give him the letter, Miss Tanner, but sometimes I'm away for two or three days on sightseeing tours. Why don't you just hand it in at the reception desk of the Taprobane?" "I have my reasons," she said. "I've got to get away from here as quickly as possible. The next plane out."

'The next day, she was hospitalised and two weeks later, after they dropped the charges for smuggling dope, she was deported to the USA. Less than a week later, she was here again. Then they killed her, and today I saw her strolling down the Janadhipathi Mawatha. What should I make of all this, Mr Kirk?'

I shrugged my shoulders. 'Have you delivered your letter yet?'

'No, I never had a chance. That Mr Kissinger never showed up. I inquired about him again and again; in the Taprobane, in Oberoi, in the Intercontinental, in the Havelock, in Galle Face – everywhere. Maybe he was detained from coming to Colombo. Perhaps someone wanted to prevent him from meeting Nancy Tanner, or she was duped into coming here and lured into a trap.' He pulled one of those rectangular tobacco pouches out of the inner pocket of his jacket. He obviously used it as a wallet. 'Lincoln-Cavendish' was printed on it in red and white. There were two sun-ripened tobacco leaves crossed like swords and a golden eagle sitting on a perch and holding the US flag in its claws. It was touchingly well-cared for, his shabby, makeshift wallet. He opened it with his thin, dark, boyish fingers and pulled out a small, lilac-coloured envelope. 'Would you be kind enough to take this letter with you to New York and give it to Mr Fred Kissinger. He lives somewhere in New York.'

'But the letter is over a month old. The message has surely been outdated by the events.'

'She writes that she can't wait any longer for him, because she feels threatened and is scared.'

'How do you know that? Did you open the letter?'

'No, of course not, but if you hold a good pocket lamp under it, you can decipher a few lines. Give the letter to Mr Kissinger and tell him what I've just told you. Tell him that something's happening to Miss Tanner and that she's fallen into the hands of Sinhalese officers who want to get revenge because of her role in the film. Tell him they are torturing and killing her and somehow or other have the power of bringing her back to life. Perhaps he can help her, perhaps he knows what's going on.'

'But what do you think I can do? What shall I say to Miss Tanner's manager?'

He did not reply, staring at the dashboard. Finally, he asked quietly, 'You don't believe me?'

I hesitated and then shook my head. 'No.' To my amazement, I noticed that he was on the verge of tears. He took off his sunglasses and wiped his eyes with his sleeves. 'I beg you to do it anyway, Mr Kirk.'

I took the envelope and put it in my pocket. Suddenly, our car was shaken by a dull thud on the roof. We started at the sound. A broad-shouldered, dark-skinned man in an overall, peaked cap and thick working gloves, motioned to us to drive on and clear the entrance. He grinned good-naturedly. The driver of the beverage truck, who had stopped diagonally behind us and who wanted to get in the driveway was honking his horn impatiently. We drove off.

'I'll take you to your hotel. It's going to rain any moment now.' We had hardly driven two hundred years when the first huge drops of rain fell on the dusty windshield.

'Shall I take you to the airport tomorrow morning?' he asked as he let me off in front of the Taprobane.

'I've got to be at the airport at seven o'clock in the morning at the latest.'

'Okay. I'll pick you up at six o'clock.'

Rain pattered against the window. Dark red flashes of lightning fell vertically into the ocean and lit up the buildings on the harbour. The gusts of rain foamed like surging billows over the roofs. I was annoyed at letting myself be talked into playing the role of postman for a ridiculous letter that was more than a month old. I really felt like handing it over to the reception without any comment at all, or just throwing it away. Perhaps one of the prostitutes at the officer's club had known how the American actress was idolised, and had dressed up to look like her in order to liven up business.

And besides, the young man had been through so much. He'd had a very serious accident on the building site, not to mention the loss of his young wife . . . Could his power of judgement be trusted? More than likely he had a lively imagination, was in love with the Tanner girl and was just fantasising it all . . . What was his name anyway? I realized angrily that I had never asked him his name. Imagine spending days with someone and only being aware of him in his function as 'our driver'. I decided to ask him his name the following morning. I packed my bag and put it beside Andrew's.

The windows trembled at the impact of the thunder.

Sheet lightning illuminated the room. My glance fell on the two pieces of luggage. I noticed for the first time that they were almost identical.

Shortly after, I must have fallen asleep.

My nameless driver was not waiting at the entrance of the Taprobane at six o'clock in the morning. The thunderstorm had moved on. The air was clear and fresh. Heaven and earth had been washed clean. The leaves shimmered – the waxen damask of the frangipani, the unreal light blue of the jacaranda, the extravagant lilac of the bougainvillea and the subdued scarlet of the hibiscus.

When the car had not yet arrived at quarter past six, I started getting nervous and asked the porter to call me another taxi. It was there in a minute. The driver looked as if he had just got out of bed. The smell of sweat was overwhelming and he constantly bored in his nose, not realizing that I could see him in his rear-view mirror. At the crossing of Prince of Wales Avenue and Madampita Road, we were caught in a traffic jam which extended all the way over Victoria Bridge. The Kelani Ganga River was on the point of clearing itself of all the junk it had accumulated. Its swelling waters were strewn with rubbish. On the shore, emaciated dogs – mere skin and bones – rummaged about for cadavers.

I looked at my watch. It was already six thirty-two. I was getting more and more nervous. It was at least twenty miles to the airport.

'Accident!' the driver said.

A soldier with white flags in his hands waved us on past the scene of the accident. A black car in an unrecognisable condition had been crushed between two heavy army trucks. A figure lay on the asphalt, covered over with dirty newspapers. I don't know all that much about European cars, but I'm almost certain it was the Peugeot of the young driver who had entrusted me with the letter.

Inspector Kirtisinghe came to me with his arms out-stretched. 'I'm so sorry, Mr Kirk. How could it have happened? I don't know any details – the report from Batticaloa has not yet arrived,' he said as if he wanted to forestall any questions from the beginning. 'What an awful fire! Poor Mr Baldenham! They certainly did everything humanly possible in the hospital. Unfortun-ately, I wasn't to be reached at the time. A bomb exploded in Puttalam. Many people were killed. How are you, Mr Kirk? Are you well?' His bright-coloured eyes were cold and without feeling. 'But why this abrupt departure? It's lovely here at this time of year. Back home, where you come from, it's cold and miserable.'

'Thank you, Inspector Kirtisinghe. I've lost all interest in taking a vacation here. I'm sure you understand.'

'Certainly, Mr Kirk. But before I wish you a good flight, I would like to return your brass knuckles.'

He reached for a dark brown paper bag which lay on the PanAm counter, broke the plastic seal and opened it. He handed me my eraser.

'Who knows, perhaps you'll need it. Have a pleasant journey, Mr Kirk!'

'Thank you.'

I handed my ticket across the counter.

'Only two bags, sir?' the ground hostess asked. She was a Sinhalese girl with large, dark, doe eyes and a velvety soft voice.

'Yes, just two.'

'Gate number five,' she said, smiling shyly as she handed me my boarding card.

'Farewell,' I said.

She nodded in that strange Asian manner, shaking her head. 'Farewell to you, sir.'

The local security officer examined my eraser suspiciously, inspecting it from all sides.

'What's this?' he asked.

'An EMPU.'

'A what?'

'Damn it all!' I shouted angrily. 'I just got that thing back from one of your security officers. And now you're starting these shenanigans all over again! What the hell do you want.'

'Sorry, sir, but I'm only following orders.'

A well-built sheriff of the PanAm boarding police pushed his way through the passengers who had already passed security control.

'It's all right,' he said to the local officer. 'You may board now, Mr Kirk.'

When I turned around again, I saw Mr Kirtisinghe standing near a fat man in a traditional Bedouin robe with a crotcheted skull cap. He seemed familiar to me. They both glanced in my direction. Then the man in the Arabian dress laughed. I saw the gold glittering in his mouth and recognised him as the one with the scarred face who had been standing at the bar of the Sultan Ahmet.

The plane was an old Airbus. Fat, meaty-looking men were resting in their seats, their haggard faces red from too much whisky – Australian sheep breeders on their way back to London on business after spending the Christmas holidays in Australia with their families.

Half an hour later, we rolled to the start. I was glad when the plane finally took off and Sri Lanka disappeared in the misty haze under us.

The stewardess handed me the *Financial Times*:

IRAN IS TESTING ITS FIRST ATOMIC BOMB PROTESTS FROM THE SOVIET UNION AND TURKEY
INDIA IS CONSIDERING CUTTING OFF DIPLOMATIC RELATIONS

Speculation continues about the scientists who made it possible for Iran to produce an atomic bomb in such a short time. Were well-known European and American scientists persuaded by the military government to work for Iran as Tass maintains? London denies that William Treholt, David Silverman or the Anglo-Indian, Lal Bhattavali have been working for Teheran. The name of the Danish Nobel Prize winner Bengt Rodestrom was also mentioned in this respect. He has allegedly retired to the Danish island of Samso.

Stopover – Bahrain. We have to get out of the plane while it is being refueled. The air-conditioning in the waiting room is running full swing. Natives dressed in robes and wrapped in blankets against the cold are sitting in deep armchairs made of black leather-grained plastic. A Pakistani with a turban and a shabby uniform jacket is emptying ash trays. Flies, accustomed to the Arctic micro-climate, are inspecting the empty cups and the coffee puddles on the tables. Postcards $5.00, stamps $5.00, coffee $5.00, tea $5.00, coca cola $5.00, Canada Dry $5.00, egg sandwich $5.00, chicken sandwich $5.00. Standard price, standard currency.

'Do you have any beer?'

The man at the bar pursed his lips, jutted his chin out and made a sound filled with indignation and loathing – tch, tch.

I look at the panoramic view from the tinted glass window. The vegetation is luxuriant due to refined ocean water, dunes can be seen in the background, naked and white like mortal remains. Bahrain – I remember the story of the young Sinhalese girl in a brothel who committed suicide out of despair and homesickness. Ugly concrete architecture, looking as if chiseled out of the filth. In the distance, luscious green and the white of palaces. Orange-coloured flames over the horizon: the flare of natural gas. Behind the dunes, the ocean glimmers an almost unreal blue. Miracle after miracle – on the wall, I discover a clock map of the world. Its shadowy curves creep over continents. The Antartic is plunged in brightness. The Arctic lies in darkness. A crude tongue of light moves from the equator up to the snow-capped Taiga between Gor'ky and Sverdlovsk. It shows daytime. The Pacific is shrouded in darkness.

In London, it's raining. The brightly coloured flags painted on the podgy snouts of the cargo aircraft of KLM, SAS and British Airways are reflected in the puddles. The Zeppelins seem to huddle together under the icy northeast sky like a pack of freezing, wet dogs.

It is late in the afternoon. The tongue of light on the clock in Bahrain is probably now licking the desolate coast of Labrador. We roll to the start on our way to New York.

Beyond Erris Head, where the Irish coast swoops down into the cool depths of the Atlantic over sombre abysses filled with the song of the last humpback whale, the night escorts us home.

7

The Hook in the Pool

It was snowing in New York and pitch dark when I got on a bus at Kennedy Airport, going to Manhattan. The driver, a grey-haired black man dressed in a warm winter coat, said: 'I'll turn the heating up a bit for you, Sir. You'll miss the sunshine. We've had a very cold Christmas here.'

'Thank you,' I said and slipped my credit card into the bus's computer slot.

A group of tourists shoved their way onto the bus. Judging from their clothes, they had also just arrived from somewhere in the sun. They were almost all blacks. It wasn't long before the bus was filled with loud music and even louder entertainment. Everyone was in a good mood. The streets we drove through were, in contrast, almost deserted.

Grand Central Station was the last stop. I asked my way to the bus heading downtown, got out at the corner of 14th and 5th Ave and went on foot to the Transfer. It was a small hotel near Washington Square, one of NASA's favourite hotels for less prominent visitors or employees on their way to Cape Canaveral or Vandenberg, the military shuttle launching areas.

'Breakfast from seven o'clock in the morning on, Sir,' the porter said and handed me my 'key', a small coded plastic card.

I had a shower and slept until almost noon. Then I bought myself some winter clothes. Later, I went into a small Italian restaurant nearby. After six months of curry, the spaghetti tasted sumptuous, the saltimbocca was a real feast, not to mention the delicious Soave wine. In the men's room, there was a sign urging all employees to wash their hands after using the toilet. I looked at my face in the small mirror over the washbasin and realized I hadn't shaved for two days.

'Can I have a data link?' I asked the porter when I got back to the hotel.

'I'll have a terminal sent up to your room immediately, Sir.'

Ten minutes later, I was sitting in front of the screen and typing my number in. The girl from infopool who, for years, had always attended to my so-called mailbox had not changed at all. She was still young, efficient and very reliable-looking. How long would it take those in charge of making computers to realize that these synthesised lovely creatures could also age naturally instead of just being dressed, hair, make-up and all, according to the latest fashion.

'Hello, Alice, how are you?'

She flashed her most beautiful smile. 'Very well, thank you, and you? Your name, date of birth and your password in a clear voice, please.'

'Peter Kirk, November 19th, 1976. Beware the Jabberwock, my son! The jaws that bite, the claws that catch! Beware the Jubjub bird and shun the frumious Bandersnatch!'

'Your voice test is positive: your password has been accepted, Mr Kirk.'

'What've we got in the mailbox today, Alice?'

'An awful lot of stuff has accumulated. As I go through it, tell me what to delete and what to leave in storage.'

'Okay, Alice, shoot!'

All of a sudden, a commercial was on the screen praising some drink that was supposed to be unbelievably refreshing and low in calories.

'Alice!'

She was on the screen again. 'What can I do for you, sir?'

'I told you to shoot!'

'If you don't want any commercials, sir, we'll have to charge you ten cents per kilobyte extra, because, as you know, a large share of infopool costs is covered by commercials.'

'I know, but no commercials for me, please!'

It was mostly unimportant stuff – bank statements, monthly bills, an inquiry from my accountant because of a non-computerised travel expense deduction, calls from friends and a few invitations to parties that had long since taken place.

There was also a greeting from Ruth. She was getting a little bit fatter, which funnily enough did wonders for her figure. She had on a tiny bikini. I could make out a swimming pool in the background. She was hugging a young boy, twenty years old if he was a day. Suntanned and in excellent shape from body-building, he was handsome enough, but his eyes were too close together which gave his face a simple, pig-headed expression. She was also tanned and wore her blonde hair straight back and somewhat shorter than she had had it before. She looked fantastic.

'Just wanted to let you know that I'm not bored without you, honey!' she says, blowing a kiss to the camera. She's obviously had a little too much to drink. She tries to give the young man a kiss on the cheek, but he looks pained and embarrassed.

She raises her glass, swaying slightly. 'Happy Birthday to you, Pete!' I glance at the date and identification code. November 19th, 2016, Fort Lauderdale.

'Delete!' I snapped.

'The next message can only be made available to you if one condition has been fulfilled, Mr Kirk.'

'What kind of condition?'

'You must confirm that no one is with you in the room at the moment.' I was surprised. It wasn't all that unusual for infopool information to be bound to a condition, especially if the news was private, confidential or of a business nature, but I was not expecting such news.

'I'm completely alone in this room, Alice,' I assured her. 'Let me see it!'

'It's just a sound recording. It's incomplete and without any identification at all and it was telephoned in. There's no sender. He must have known the priority code, otherwise the computer would not have accepted it. Infopool never accepts any anonymous messages.'

I had to hold on to the table with both hands when I heard Andrew's voice suddenly saying, 'Pete, I can't reach Andrew. Please tell him if he's still alive that someone called whose voice sounded exactly like his. He'll know what's going on. Tell him that someone's carrying on Roughtrade's . . . ' The voice died off. The mechanical tone of a broken telephone connection was heard, unnaturally loud. I sat there, thunderstruck. What did he mean? It was definitely Andrew's voice. Exhausted, under stress, almost a little nervous, but definitely Andrew's voice.

'When was this message sent in?'

'No date on it, Mr Kirk, but it was channeled into the pool on December 25th.'

Christmas day.

'Any other messages?'

'Yes, another message. It was channeled into the pool in a similar manner on December 27th. A sound recording again – no sender, no identification.'

And it was Andrew's voice again!

'Listen, Pete! I don't know if I'll have another chance to contact you so soon – to find a telephone or if I'm being watched at this moment making this phone call. As I don't know whether I'm still living or not, I've contacted you too to be on the safe side. I don't know if this is the first message you've received from me or if you've received several by now? Collect them in chronological order and keep them ready for retrieval for me in a demand file! This will all seem very confusing and unreal, but do what I say! Contact Kenneth Buchan, Head of National Security immediately. He'll explain everything to you if he thinks it's necessary. Tell him I have proof that someone is carrying on Roughtrade's business. Be careful! There could be a hook in the pool that reacts to his name. I think I'm still in Sri Lanka, but it's possible that further mes . . . '

'The message stopped there, Mr Kirk!'

'Is . . . is there any other message like that one for me, Alice?'

'No, nothing else in the mailbox, sir.'

What was happening? What kind of obscure messages were these? Was Andrew not really dead after all? Absolute nonsense! I had been to the morgue to identify his corpse. There was no doubt about it. Of course he was dead. *'As I don't know whether I'm still living or not . . . '* What was that supposed to mean? It was definitely his voice. But voices are easy to synthesise if there are a sufficient number of recordings of the original. Was someone playing a macabre joke on him? What else could it be? Andrew was dead. It was definitely his corpse that I had seen, his mutilated body. *'I think I'm still in Sri Lanka . . . '*

'Do you need me anymore, Mr Kirk?'

'Oh, sorry, Alice, no, thank you . . . um, yes. I'd like you to do two things for me. Put those last two messages ready for retrieval in a demand file for Andrew Baldenham. And then send the following message to

Kenneth Buchan: Andrew Baldenham told me that he has proof that someone is carrying on Roughtrade's business, whatever that means. He also said that you would explain all this to me. That is, Andrew's voice told me all this. Andrew Baldenham himself is dead. He died on December 23rd in the army hospital in Colombo. End – thanks, Alice.'

'It was my pleasure, Mr Kirk.'

Alice disappeared from the screen.

I stared out of the window. It was still snowing. The towers of the World Trade Center were shrouded in clouds. I stared at the building next to ours – a dreary-looking piece of architecture made of what had once been red brick and was now blackened by soot. Its cornices, crusted over with pigeon shit, and its rusty fire escapes had been transformed by the snow into a Brussels' lace filigree. On the next floor down, a church service was obviously in progress. The minister was standing directly in front of the window, gesticulating solemnly. He was wearing a hideous blue and red checkered jacket and kept running his hand over what little hair he had left. Now and then, stormy applause could be heard. Suddenly, he tore his jacket off furiously and hurled it to the ground in a rage. Then, he turned his back to his audience, folded his arms and scowled up at me. I instinctively turned away.

I knew that there were some people who delighted their relatives with birthday and holiday wishes long after their death, or who scared them with macabre phone calls from the hereafter – messages that had been stored in infopools with a timeout command. But Andrew definitely wasn't the type to indulge in such tasteless jokes. Whoever it was must have been well-informed. Or . . . ? Not really. Our stay in Sri Lanka and the fact that Kenneth Buchan was Head of National Security at NASA were both common knowledge.

I turned the computer on again.

'Hello, Alice, how are you?'

She smiled another one of her charming smiles. 'Very well, thank you, and you? Name, date of birth and your password in a clear voice, please.'

'You're a dreadfully forgetful young girl, Alice. Don't you remember our long chat – why it was hardly a quarter of an hour ago!'

'I know, Mr Kirk, but I'm only following regulations.'

We repeated the whole procedure.

'Alice, I would like to hear the last two messages again.'

'Yes, sir.'

I let them run through twice. If they were phony, then they were brilliantly done. They were both slightly impaired because they had been transmitted by phone, but as far as the voice was concerned, it had more than one pitch, almost impossible to achieve by synthesising. *'Be careful! There could be a hook in the pool that reacts to the name . . . '* Roughtrade. Andrew had mentioned the name. He had even talked about a Roughtrade machine with which one could reproduce things. *Like the fairy-tales: Magic Table! Gold Donkey! Club in the Sack!* Hadn't he mentioned Rumpelstiltskin? Straw turned into gold?

The MIDAS project? Midas was a king of the ancient Greeks, whose wish that everything he touched be turned to gold was fulfilled by the gods, and who then almost died of hunger as the food he touched also turned to gold. Molecular Integrating and Digital Assembling System. A system with which one could integrate and build molecules from digital information. Was it a secret government project for research on bio-computers? Top specialists in chaos research were certainly involved – determinists on the one hand, randomists on the other. According to the determinists, nothing happens by chance – everything is linked to cause and effect, everything calculable, predetermined from the beginning of time. According to the randomists, chance rules world affairs. Nothing is predetermined or regulated – everything is an interplay of probabilities. There are always alternative possibilities. Chaos is real. Causality is only a habit of thinking – a result of the structure of the human brain.

MIDAS – the basis of Multimanna. 'Magic Table', okay. But, Gold Donkey, Club in the Sack? What did he mean by it all. I don't know much about fairy tales. I'll have to do some reading up on them when I have a chance.

Didn't he mention a bomb in connection with multi-manna? To bomb hunger from the world? Synthetic protein?

'Do you believe in the resurrection of the flesh?'

'No, Andrew, I don't believe in it.'

'Do you need me anymore, Mr Kirk?'

'Yes, Alice. Please send a message to Andrew Baldenham as follows: Dear Andrew, I don't believe in the resurrection of the flesh or in life after death. I can't accept such a form of comfort. Best wishes, Pete. End – thank you, Alice. Is there no answer from Kenneth Buchan yet?'

'No, Mr Kirk. Mr Buchan is in a meeting. Only messages marked "urgent" are being transmitted to his wrist terminal.'

'It *is* urgent!'

'You forgot to tell me that, Mr Kirk.'

'Can't you just add "urgent" to the message now?'

'Unfortunately not, but you can repeat the message, of course, and then send it a second time with the entry "urgent". Would you like me to do that, Mr Kirk?'

'Oh, forget it, Alice. Please find me the address of Mr Fred Kissinger, here in New York.'

'Frederic or Alfred Kissinger?'

'Ah . . . I don't know.'

'There are about sixteen Frederic or Albert Kissingers in New York.'

'I mean the film director.'

'Just a moment – he lives at 42 West 125th Street, 8th floor.'

'Is he in New York at the moment?'

'I don't have permission to give you that information. Shall I send him a message?'

'No, Alice, I'll take a walk over to his place. I have something real old-fashioned in my pocket – you won't believe it – a letter! Would you like to come with me, Alice?'

She beamed another one of her lovely smiles.

'I identify that as a joke, although I don't understand it. I don't need to go anywhere – I AM everywhere. I hope you're satisfied with me, Mr Kirk?'

'You're a wonderful girl, Alice!'

I was freezing in spite of my winter coat, and my new shoes were pinching, but I continued stubbornly on foot.

It snowed incessantly. There was a lot of traffic, but the noise seemed strangely hushed and very far away.

I passed the gruesome ruins of the Plaza, where international terrorists had succeeded in ringing in the new millennium. I was a student at CalTech at the time. The monstrous event was shown live on TV. It was New Year's Eve 1999 and a grand banquet was in full swing at the Plaza with over a thousand guests. High society, including all the east coast millionaires, had gathered to celebrate New Year's Eve and ring in the third millennium. During the banquet, a Palestinian terrorist commando had stormed the hotel and taken all those present as hostages. There were differences of opinion as to how many terrorists were involved, and the exact number was never determined, but it must have been an organised body of at least fifty men. They demanded ten billion dollars and the President's promise that the people of Palestine receive their own country.

At first, it looked as if the Palestinians would succeed in at least getting the ten billion dollars. Among the hostages there were several Governors, more than a dozen Senators, Members of Congress, many close friends of the President and a lot of influential people from the financial world, industry and the press. Malicious tongues contended that those people were capable of paying ten times the amount to set themselves free. When President Newbury declared however – and it was really meant as a joke – that he had begged the Prime Minister of England to give the Falklands over to the Palestinians, the terrorists lost their patience. They started hurling a hostage every hour from the top floor of the Plaza to the street below and they chose Members of Congress, Senators and Governors as their first victims. The gruesome show was shown on TV round the clock and transmitted all over the world via satellite. More than two billion people sat in front of their television sets and, whenever a body smashed to pieces on the asphalt below and the cameramen zoomed it onto the screen, a cry of indignation shook the American nation. This, at least, was Newbury's version later (which didn't prevent a few from saying that those who deserved it finally got their dues). In short, Newbury offered his Blue Lights to storm the Plaza. The rest was pure horror! The terrorists made their threat come true and blew themselves, the hostages and the Plaza up. Fewer than a hundred hostages survived the inferno. The ruins were left standing as a gruesome reminder. The fact was that the district between Central Park and Grand Central Station had in the meantime become one of the seediest and most dangerous slums in the USA. The fashionable apartment buildings and the luxury hotels were scraping the skies in the Bronx and

Harlem, north of 116th Street, where Fred Kissinger lived.

Three cameras and the submachine gun of a police-man turned in my direction, while a second policeman checked my identity and had me announced. The sub-machine gun motioned me to the elevator.

'Go up, but don't try to stop anywhere on your way up, mister!'

Fred Kissinger was waiting at the door of his apart-ment. He was a rather short man, anywhere from sixty to sixty-five years old. He had had the sideburns of his medium-length white hair dyed a sandy colour. His cheeks and lips were discreetly made up. He was probably much older than he appeared at first glance. He was wearing a pair of yellow-tinted glasses, which made it hard to see his eyes. His white towelling bathrobe had red braiding around the edges and there was a hand-embroidered red Chinese dragon on the left-hand breast pocket. Its long tail wound itself around its body.

'To what do I owe this honour, Mr Kirk? Please come in! I don't believe we've ever met before.'

'No, I've never met you officially, Mr Kissinger, but I know who you are and have seen several films of yours.'

He dismissed the discussion disparagingly with a wave of his hand. I noticed that he was wearing a ring with an enormous star sapphire on the middle finger of his left hand.

His rooftop apartment was enormous, maisonette style and luxuriously furnished with antique Japanese cupboards and tables inlaid with selected wood, mother-of-pearl and silver. Chinese porcelain and jade carvings that must have cost a fortune were displayed in plexiglass showcases. Antique shadow-play figures were artistically arranged over one wall. The terrace was almost completely glassed in and overgrown with tropical plants. There were at least a dozen different kinds of orchids.

'I've been cultivating orchids for almost forty years now,' he said as he followed my glance. 'They're the loveliest and most vulnerable creatures in the world! Would you like a drink?'

'Oh . . . no – no, thank you.'

'Please excuse my attire, but I've taken on the custom of that old philosopher – was it Descartes or Erasmus of Rotterdam – who never left his bed in winter and even received his visitors in his bed chamber because he abhorred the cold. Thanks to modern-day electronic equipment, it's no longer necessary to leave one's house. I absolutely refuse to go out during the winter months.' He smiled, but it was difficult to say whether his eyes were friendly because of his tinted glasses. Probably not. I didn't like the man, no matter how friendly and open-minded he pretended to be, no matter how intellectual and artistic he actually was.

'I have a letter for you from Miss Tanner. I brought it with me from Colombo.'

'Oh,' he said raising his eyebrows. 'Good old Nancy always had a romantic streak in her. Who writes letters nowadays?'

He seemed a bit annoyed. I handed him the thin envelope. His hands shook a little as he accepted it. 'It's her handwriting all right. Who gave it to you?'

'A taxi driver gave it to me and he asked me . . . '

'A taxi driver?' He seemed relieved at the news. 'And where did he get it from?'

'From Miss Tanner personally. She gave it to him a month ago when she was in Colombo.'

He seemed even more relieved. He was obviously in no hurry to open it. 'I know what this is all about and it's already been settled. Nancy's on the way to recovery.

She'd been snuffing a lot of that hot stuff. I phone her every day in the hospital. Were you there as a tourist in Colombo?'

'Yes, I . . . I was on vacation there for a couple of days.'

'There aren't many tourists there anymore.'

'That's right.'

'Where are you staying in New York?' he asked casually.

'With a friend over in Queens.' I don't know why, but I felt I was better off lying to him.

'Thank you, Mr Kirk, for all the trouble you went to – playing the mailman. How romantic,' he said, putting his arm around my shoulder on the way to the door. 'How lovely of you to do such a thing in this unemotional age. Goodbye, Mr Kirk.'

It was already dark when I walked back to my hotel through Central Park. It had stopped snowing. The snow lay virgin white. The park was almost deserted.

'NASA has been trying to reach you for hours, Mr Kirk! Where have you been?' the porter asked, completely flustered.

'Is the terminal still in my room?'

'No, not on infopool. We have a special hot-line to NASA here. Please take the call in the visaphone booth over there. I'll connect you right away!'

Kenneth Buchan didn't have the usual stocky stature of most security officers. He was a small man, almost slight in fact, but his voice, used to issuing commands, was loud and his glance so full of authority it made him look at least three inches taller.

'You're out galavanting around as cool as you please, while I spend my time searching for you like a needle in a haystack,' he thundered out. 'Whatever gave you the idea that you could just go roaming about without leaving a message?'

'Sir, I was out for a walk . . . '

'No one in his right mind goes out for a walk any-more, especially in Manhattan!'

'Pardon me, sir, but that's my business.'

'No, it isn't your business, damn it all!'

'Sir . . . '

'Listen, Kirk! You let Roughtrade's name go through the infopool. You know how hot his name is and there's sure to be a hook that's speared it by now. God knows what alarm it's set ringing. Now pay attention, Kirk! You could be in danger. Get your luggage and take a taxi to Kennedy Airport! Take the next plane to Fort Lauderdale or Miami. I want you here at Cape Canaveral. I want a first-hand account of this Baldenham story, do you understand? It stinks to high heaven! Leave the hotel immediately. Don't have them call a taxi! Get out on the street and flag one! Do you understand?'

'Okay, Mr Buchan. But I don't understand why I should be in danger!'

'I'll tell you everything when you're here. End!'

I took the elevator up to my room and packed my things. When I got back to the lobby, I looked in the mirror on the opposite wall and saw two men standing at the reception. They both had on heavy winter coats and hats and were not carrying any luggage. I heard my name and slipped quietly into the toilet leaving the door open just a crack.

'He's up in his room,' the porter was telling them.

'What number?'

'312. Hey, where are you going?'

'We want to visit him.'

'Just a moment – I'll tell him that you're here.'

'It's not necessary. He's expecting us.' They got into the elevator. The porter picked up the house telephone.

'Don't bother!' I said.

'Two gentlemen wanted to talk to you, Mr Kirk. They're on their way upstairs.'

'Say hello to them for me! Tell them I've gone out for a walk as trouble is brewing in the air here.'

'What do you mean by that?'

'You're not meant to know what it means! NASA's decisions are unfathomable, but usually very wise. They need me for a flight to Mars.'

'Shall I call a taxi, Mr Kirk?'

'No, thanks. I'm in a hurry. Perhaps you could stall those boys for a while! Bye.'

8

Messages from the Living and the Dead

An icy wind was blowing at Cape Canaveral. It rippled the waters of the lagoon. The tops of the palm trees shook morosely, hissing like startled rattlesnakes.

'We lost eighty percent of the citrus crop to the cold last week,' Buchan said, 'and the alligators were slower than ever. You could've hit them with an iron rod and they wouldn't have reacted.'

A cloud of steam rose from the launch pad, then an orange-red fire flared up. The Friday shuttle took off and, thundering and seething, took the sky by storm, burning out the thin covering of clouds with its flickering tongue of flames. Buchan turned away from the window.

He was a small wiry man with lively eyes and a physical presence so pronounced that it lent him an aura of natural authority. His ancestors must certainly have been Italians and his elegant dress confirmed this impression. He was wearing a light grey-blue suit and a complementary dark blue tie. His shoes, made of soft brown leather, were obviously expensive.

'Sit down, Peter,' he said, gesturing towards a chair. 'You said you had a right to know what's happening.' He folded his arms behind his head and regarded me with his dark eyes. 'Well, you don't, Pete. Just put that idea out of your head. The less you know the better! It's for your own personal safety, Pete. However, one thing

I can tell you – your friend, Andrew Baldenham is dead. He was my friend, too, you know. He is dead, a sad but irrevocable fact. I'm not sure whether he wasn't intentionally killed. There is every indication not only from the circumstances, but also from the way you described the events, that it was an accident.'

'Accident? Listen! That night . . . '

' . . . an accident happened. But the fire wasn't an accident. They staged it *after* Andrew had lost his lower legs in another accident. You yourself said that the sudden appearance of soldiers, a doctor and the hasty evacuation of Andrew by helicopter seemed rather suspect.'

'Do you mean to say that he was dragged out of the hotel and taken somewhere and that then his . . . ?'

'Yes, I presume that he was overwhelmed in his sleep and abducted to the military base nearby.'

'But why?'

Buchan hesitated for a moment and bit his bottom lip. Then he said resolutely, 'To make a recording of him.'

'A *what*?'

'A recording. Andrew Baldenham is dead. But there's an electronic recording of him. It was the recording that got in touch with you.'

'You mean Andrew's brain is stuck in some stupid computer?'

'I'm not a specialist when it comes to computers, but I suppose you could put it that way.'

'How could such a thing be technically possible?'

'Don't ask me, Pete. The fact is that Andrew and another scientist from CalTech developed this procedure in a secret project directed by Professor Roughtrade. It goes without saying that this information is top secret and that you're not, under any circumstances, allowed to pass it on to anyone.'

'Andrew said that the project had failed and that they stopped all research on it.'

'Yes and no. The recording procedure didn't work properly and they weren't able to improve it beyond an inadequate degree of accuracy. In the end, they were convinced that the source of error could not be eliminated. So, this project, in which we at NASA had such great faith, was dropped.'

'How could such a project have been of any value to space research?'

'One could have sent unmanned missiles with the appropriate receiving equipment on board into space and years later, at the speed of light, the necessary scientists.'

'As recordings?'

'Yes, as recordings – while the original person remained here on earth.'

'And when the recordings were no longer needed, they could be deleted.'

'Right, they could be deleted.'

Buchan stood up and went over to the window. The wind had blown the cloud of steam and smoke southwards and dispersed it.

'Who would want to make recordings of people if the recordings are not good?'

'The security regulations for the MIDAS project obviously left much to be desired. Important documents fell into the wrong hands. Someone's earning a hell of a lot of money making recordings of top scientists and selling them to interested buyers, especially in the Third World.'

'Roughtrade's business.'

'Right, Roughtrade's business.'

The idea was breathtaking.

'Have these recordings been used on others? There were the Torre and Rodestrom doubles . . . '

'Unfortunately, but we don't have the least bit of proof,' Buchan said over his shoulder. 'However, who knows, the procedure could have been perfected in the meantime.'

'In his message, Andrew said – that is, the recording of Andrew – that he didn't know when he'd be able to get to a telephone again and just how long he could remain unobserved.'

Buchan shrugged his shoulders. 'He might have meant that figuratively.'

MIDAS – Molecular Integrating and Digital Assembling System – the basis for Multimanna.

'What does "Multimanna" mean?'

Buchan whirled around. 'What did Andrew tell you about Multimanna?'

'He said literally: "Magic Table! Gold Donkey! Club in the Sack!"'

Buchan nodded, then he burst out laughing. 'That would have been the next step if the determinists had had their way – the retranslation of signals into matter or as the theorists put it, the conversion of signals from the electronic media into matter. However, they never got that far.'

Peter, do you believe in the resurrection of the flesh?

He shrugged his shoulders. 'It was a scientific deadlock, even though there were a few scientists who didn't want to admit it. Imagine such people – the so-called elite of science – worrying about their image, their careers. What vanity and foolishness!' He snorted disdainfully. 'You technicians are so reliable in comparison.'

'What do you mean by that, sir?'

The terminal on Buchan's wrist began to blink. He held it to his ear and replied, 'Tell George I'll be there in ten minutes.'

He took his camel hair coat out of the closet and put it on.

'Have your medical check-up today, Pete. I'd like you

to go up with the shuttle on Tuesday. There's a lot of work to be done up there. It'll give you something else to think about.'

'Something else to think about, Sir?'

He stopped in the middle of buttoning up his coat. 'I'm sure Andrew's death has grieved you tremendously.'

'Yes, he was my friend.'

Buchan nodded. 'Contact infopool every day. Should Andrew's copy send another message, send it to me immediately on a NASA line.'

'Yes, Sir.'

'Can I give you a lift part of the way?'

'No, thank you, Sir. The short walk to the team's quarters will do me good.'

'You seem to be very fond of walking.'

'Yes, all of us who've been in orbit for a long time are fond of walking, you know. One forgets how to walk up there . . . Walking is a great . . . For me, that is.'

He seemed not to be listening, turned up the collar of his coat, fished the computer card for his car out of an elegant leather bag and said, 'The day after tomorrow is New Year's Eve, Pete. But don't celebrate too much – the doctors don't approve of it at all, especially just before takeoff.'

'Okay, Sir. In case we don't see each other again, may I wish you a Happy New . . . ?'

'No, don't, I'm terribly superstitious!'

He raised his hand in farewell.

I was really annoyed at his arrogance, but even more so at myself, because I had stooped to wish him a Happy New Year!

Outside, the wind hit me. It hounded over the concrete and ripped angrily at the evergreen hedges like an invisible pack of wolves.

I blew into my hands and pulled my coat tighter around me. When I arrived at the team's quarters, I saw a tall, heavy-built man unloading large brown grocery bags from his Dodge. He wore a pearl grey Stetson – large enough for twelve rabbits – and white studded cowboy boots. He was sweating in spite of the cold. He pushed his hat back and wiped his forehead. His red hair was short and greying at the temples. He opened the door and put his foot between the door and the threshold. He stopped when he saw me and he put the heavy bags down carefully. There was a clinking of bottles.

'You must be Peter Kirk,' he said and grinned. There were gaps between his teeth. They looked like white tiles stuck into his gums. 'Charles Cadigan,' he said and shook hands. His hand was like a giant paw.

'I hear you're taking over for me on the Tuesday shuttle. I'm going up a week from now. Thanks to you, I can really enjoy the New Year's Eve party.' He pointed with a nod in the direction of the bags. 'Why don't you join us. I've invited all the orbit people down here to come.'

'If the doctor doesn't have any objections, I'd love to. Thanks for the invitation.'

'Promise?' He nodded encouragingly.

'Promise!'

The check-up took more than three hours. The computer had to compare the results with previous tests and analyse them. I had lost eight pounds in the tropics, probably due to all the excitement of the past few days. Was it really only a week ago?

After a couple of dozen rounds in the centrifuge with sensors and feedback devices stuck all over me, I massaged the stubborn marks from my skin and showered the sweat of exhaustion from my body. I was really out of condition and thankful for every pound I had lost.

Then the tailors had a go at me. They brought James

in. I patted him on his padded shoulders like an old friend. The helmet plate had a fresh coat of gold and gleamed like a Christmas tree decoration.

A few alterations were necessary, but four hours later James was like the lap of Abraham, hugging me like a second skin with the familiar stink of my own body.

'Hello, James,' I said. 'Home again. How are you old skin?'

'All functions okay.'

'Is that all you feel?'

'All functions okay.'

I gave the thumbs up sign. The tailor nodded and began to peel James off.

The apartment assigned to me had air conditioning, but no heating. I sat down on the bed, wrapped a horrible quilt with yellow and green flowers on it around me, pulled the terminal closer to the bed and made sure something to drink was within easy reach.

The mailbox was empty.

'What is a Rumpelstiltskin, Alice?'

'Would you kindly spell that out for me, Mr Kirk? Rumpel or Rumple . . . ?'

'I've no idea. I've only heard the word – never seen it written.'

'Then I'll have to give it an etymological run, Mr Kirk. It'll take a while. May I show you a film in the meantime? I've a recent NASA publication that would interest you – "SPS to EFOS: 1976 to 2016 – Forty Years of US Space Travel for Peace".'*

'God, no, thank you, Alice!'

'But I've a note in your file that you're interested in space activities.'

'Yes, certainly. But that's my job, Alice. And next

---

* SPS: Satellite Power System. A study of Energy Satellites from the '70s of the 20th Century.

week I'll be in orbit again to see for myself what they're building nowadays.'

'Sorry, Mr Kirk.'

'You don't need to be sorry, Alice. Show me what you've found in the meantime.'

RUMPLE appeared on the screen. – CREASE, WRINKLE, CRUMPLE, FOLD MDu. ROMPEL, derivative of MDu ROMPE, MLG. RUMPE, MDU MLG RUMPELEN, ROMPELEN

'Seems to indicate that the word is of German or Dutch origin, the ending as well.'

Sentences rippled over the screen and suddenly came to a halt.

RUMPELN – RUMBLE, RATTLE, MAKE A RACKET > rummel > rumpel > rumpelkammer, rumpelkasten (> Geruempel – junk) > RUMPELSTILTSKIN (German RUMPELSTILZCHEN; Dutch REPELSTEELTJE) fairy tale figure. RUMPEL: MLG for poltergeist, noisy goblin. STILTSKIN: MLG: dim of (old) Stilt, Stuelz, Stilzer = hobble > STELZE > STILTZ > STELLEN > STOLZ

'There we have it! It's a German word and the title of a fairy tale that was originally German.'

'You're brilliant, Alice!'

Now, she ought to look flattered with a somewhat embarrassed smile. But her smile was too professional. The software designers haven't caught the knack of programming spontaneous reactions.

The following appeared on the screen:

> GRIMM, WILHELM & JACOB FAIRY TALES, ed. 1812 ref. WILD, HENRIETTE DOROTHEA, 1811

Andrew had always been interested in such things. He was unbelievably well-educated. He had a knowledge of fairy tales from all over the world. He spoke German, Spanish, French and Italian as well as a little Arabic, Turkish and Tamil. He had a brain like a computer – stored full of thousands of books.

'I don't know much about fairy tales, Alice. Do you have a recording of this one?'

'There's a Disney Production cartoon version and a 3-D computer version by Gremlins Inc.'

'Read me the text only!'

The infopool still worked on short-term memory with laser discs. Long-term memory, where all important literature, art and other basic data on the civilisation of mankind are stored, had long since switched to ULT crystals. This memory, cooled to almost zero Kelvin, has a millionfold storage capacity, but correspondingly longer access. It took Alice more than two minutes to find the text.

'Once upon a time there was a poor miller who had a beautiful daughter . . . '

A strange story. A loud-mouthed miller pompously assures his king that his daughter can spin straw to gold. The king being greedy – what king isn't – employs the girl. He puts her to work immediately at the spinning wheel. She must produce, under pain of death. The girl fulfils her father's promise, but only because a hobgoblin comes to her rescue. This makes her doubly dependent. In order to escape death and become Queen, she finally promises him her first child. When the time comes to pay her debt, she causes such a fuss that the hobgoblin agrees to let her off if she can guess his name. She does, by some bizarre coincidence, and the hobgoblin flies into a rage and tears himself to pieces.

What had Andrew meant when he talked about transforming straw into gold? Perhaps, in a figurative sense – easy money? Gold . . . Midas! The reason for the secret name . . . Roughtrade? But the name Roughtrade was not a secret. True, it was dangerous to mention the name to the data network. A hobgoblin with magic powers, who in the end flies into a rage and tears himself to pieces? No, it didn't make sense.

'Is there a fairytale with the title, "Magic Table! Gold Donkey! Club in the Sack" – or something similar?'

'Just a moment.'

> GRIMM, WILHELM & JACOB FAIRY TALES, ed. 1812 ref: A:
HASSENPFLUG, Johanna Isabella 1812, B: WILD, Henriette
Dorothea, 1811

'It's in the same collection as the first one. There's a
Disney Production cartoon version and two computer
productions by . . . '

'Just read the text, please, Alice!'

The story was even more abstruse. A cantankerous
tailor drives his three sons from home because he
chooses to believe the lies of a wicked goat rather than
his sons' assurances to the contrary. The youths –
somewhat naive, but very industrious – set off into the
world to make their fortune. The eldest son becomes a
carpenter and, as a going away present from his master,
receives a magic table that spreads itself with delicious
food. The second is apprenticed to a miller and is given
a donkey that spews forth shining gold pieces. The third
becomes a lathe-worker and his master makes him a
present of a sack with a magic club in it, which, on
commmand, whips out and beats up anyone who
deserves to be attacked. A thievish innkeeper exchanges
the presents of the first two sons for a table and a
donkey without any magic qualities, and the sons make
fools of themselves in front of their relatives who gather
to marvel at their fortune. But, with his magic club, the
third son recovers the real table and donkey from the
innkeeper and brings them home to everyone's delight.

'Is that all, Alice?'

'That's all.'

The same subject again – how to make gold. Gold out
of straw. Gold instead of dung droppings. Reminiscences
of alchemy. The government of the United States would
never spend a penny on a project whose main aim was
to produce gold. So that was easy money! Money like
dirt, money from dirt. MIDAS.

*   *   *

Magic Table: *A bomb . . . we could have bombed hunger from the world.* Multimanna?

Club in the Sack – calculated violence. Peacemaker – the club as a moral authority? Hardly – no, this wasn't getting me anywhere.

'Do you need me anymore, Mr Kirk?'

'Sorry, Alice, no. If you ever lose your job at Infopool, I'll hire you as my personal fairy tale teiler – okay? When I was a child, no one ever had time to tell me fairy tales. I've got a lot to make up for.'

'I don't know how I should interpret that, Mr Kirk.'

'What a shame! Forget it, Alice!'

On Saturday afternoon, the mailbox was still empty.

'Who's Cecil Roughtrade?' I asked Alice straight out. I felt I was safe enough in Cape Canaveral.

'I'm afraid the present tense is not correct, Mr Kirk. Mr Cecil Roughtrade is dead.'

'Since when?'

'He died on April 26th, 2004 in a car accident, south-east of Santa Monica.'

'What was he?'

'A physicist. His field of research was the storage of information in ultra low temperature crystal lattices. He was the director of a secret government project for eight years. It was discontinued shortly before his death.'

'MIDAS?'

'It was a secret project, Mr Kirk. I have no access to information catalogued as secret.'

'Do you have a picture of him?'

A tall thin man with rimless glasses appeared on the screen. He was clean-shaven and had slightly curly blond hair. His face was soft and friendly. He was wearing a light custom-made suit with a waistcoat and an unobtrusive red and white patterned tie. A likeable, pleasant person. He raised his hand as if he were greeting someone to the left of the camera. The gesture, in spite of its sincerity, seemed rather shy. Was he waving to his wife? An acquaintance? A girlfriend?

'Was he married?'

'Yes, and divorced in 2003. Two daughters.'

'Male friends?'

'That was insinuated now and again.'

So he was homosexual. One of those well-mannered young men from a good home. Not an athlete. Probably teased and sexually blackmailed by the college rowdies. His marriage, set up by his overly protective parents, was, in spite of good intentions, doomed to failure. He had sought recognition in the field of science. A brilliant theory – a fantastic career with the possibility of highest honours. An ambitious government project – another failure – his theory couldn't be proved mathematically. Sneering laughter from his fellow scientists, cancellation of funds . . .

'Did he commit suicide?'

'There was an investigation and some doubt as to whether it had been his own fault. The official decision was "human failure".'

'Why, if this man has been dead for more than twelve years, is there a hook in the pool baiting the name of Roughtrade, Alice?'

'Unfortunately, I can't give you any information . . . '

'But there is a hook in the pool.'

'Is that a question or a statement of fact, Mr Kirk?'

'A statement of fact.'

'Okay. Had you asked a question, I wouldn't have been in a position to answer it.'

'Is the statement of fact correct?'

'I cannot answer your question.'

'Why not?'

'If you mean by a hook a phonetic or optic sensor, which reacts to a determined series of sounds or letters that run through the infopool, then you are talking about protective measures that can only be ordered by the highest national or international security.'

'No misuse possible?'

'Misuse absolutely impossible.'

'Hmm. If the security officials at NASA are right, such a hook almost cost me my life as it had obviously been misused by someone.'

'I'm sorry about that, Mr Kirk.'

'That's really kind of you, Alice.'

'Do you think that it was misuse?'

'I have no other explanation.'

'If you wish – I'll send your conjecture on to be investigated, Mr Kirk.'

'You do that, Alice, old girl. But why would there be a hook for the name of a man who no longer exists?'

'I have no access to information like that.'

'Come on, Alice.'

'You seem to forget, Mr Kirk, that I'm just following instructions. I'm a machine.'

'Don't let them fool you, Alice. You're the most charming software I've ever met.'

'Nice of you to say so, Mr Kirk.'

'If they ever make an electronic recording of me like the one they've made of Mr Baldenham, I'll see to it that we meet in your world, Alice!'

It was pure vanity on my part, but I thought she hesitated slightly. I interpreted it as embarrassment. But it didn't take her long to answer, 'That would be nice, Mr Kirk.'

I accepted Charles Cadigan's invitation. The guests were all from orbit – mostly the construction crew. A few of them had worked on Sunbird 2 and Sunbird 3. I knew them only by sight.

There was a lot of heavy drinking. Unfortunately, the nine of us destined to go up with the Tuesday shuttle – six men and three women – had been put on a strict alcohol limit. And, as is usually the case when the others can let their hair down and you can't, I never got into the party mood. I couldn't help thinking about Andrew. Had they really succeeded in making a copy of him, in storing his brain? Buchan was convinced that it must've happened that night in Batticaloa. But how, when nothing, to my knowledge, had ever been published on the subject. But that didn't mean anything. Attempts to transfer neuralgic impulses to the interface of a computer had been made in the '80s of the last century, but they had never succeeded with a direct exchange of ideas or a transfer of the actual contents of the brain. Had there ever been secret projects of this kind that had been more successful?

Even if it were possible – and the more I thought about it, the less I doubted it all – what would it be like to be stuck fully conscious in a computer, in a cage made of crystals, wires and chips? Did one have a physical presence? Did one feel pain, sorrow or grief? What was the electronic equivalent of love, of friendship? A new state of mind? A new form of life?

'Happy New Year, Andrew!'

It was long after midnight when I looked for the men's room. I opened the door and fumbled for the light switch. A sound in the darkness made me stop. It was a trembling subdued sigh – 'Ah . . . ah . . . ah . . . ah . . . ' The light from the corridor fell into the room and I could make out two figures wedged tightly together, a pale behind pumping.

'Heh, you idiot!' one of them, obviously the man, panted without stopping, 'don't pee here on the wall! The john is one door down!'

'Excuse me,' I murmured, withdrawing to the corridor and closing the door.

The toilet was occupied. Someone was throwing up pitifully. I went to the front of the house and watered the evergreen shrubs near the driveway. Orion was right above me at its zenith. With glittering epaulets on his sloping shoulders and his diamond-studded sword-belt, he stood straddle-legged above me like a Caudillo of the galaxy. The night air was warmer, or was I just imagining it?

'Seems to be getting warmer,' my host appeared and planted himself beside me to relieve himself, too.

'Some of your guests seem to be really enjoying themselves,' I said, closing my zipper.

He raised his head and laughed. 'We're a wild bunch down here. But you can't blame them. After all, we live like trappists in orbit for months on end.'

'I'll have to be off now, I'm afraid. I've got an appointment with the witch doctors at ten o'clock in the morning.'

'If we don't see each other again – have a good flight!' He pointed with his head to the sky. 'See you up there soon.'

'And thanks for the invitation, Charlie.'

'Good night!'

When I arrived back from the training centre on Sunday evening, the mailbox was still empty – not even the unavoidable courtesy call from Ruth. Perhaps she was still asleep.

'Happy New Year, Alice!'

'Same to you, Mr Kirk.'

I was dead beat. I drank two cans of beer and, before solitude could overcome me, fell fast asleep. I dreamed I was in a hall full of machines – hundreds of them all working in hushed silence. Roughtrade was there dressed in an elegant light-grey single-breasted suit with a blue and white patterned tie. He pointed in his unassuming manner to a sort of punch press. The severed rump and legs of a donkey loomed out of the machine. The donkey's asshole had been obscenely enlarged with a **metal bolt. Each time the bolt was pulled down, a** sparkling gold coin would shoot out and fall to the ground. A stack of coins, almost ankle deep, had already piled up. The bolt, activated by a strong spring, snapped back into the asshole, while the legs jerked in silent animal pain. Nauseated, I turned to Roughtrade, who, smiling shyly, was trying to explain how the hideous mechanism worked. But his voice was as mute as all the machines. Terrified, I pressed both my hands to my ears, frightened that I had become deaf.

At this point in the dream, I awoke. Day had dawned. I went to the window. There, on the other side of the lagoon, the Tuesday shuttle, bathed in gleaming light, rolled to the launch pad. It hung there between the two booster rockets on the accessory unit like a pale lifeless moth. Red lights were blinking. A siren wailed.

On Monday, I looked into the mailbox again.

'He took his vorpal sword in hand: Long time the manxome foe he sought – So rested he by the Tumtum tree and stood awhile in thought.'

'Excuse me, Mr Kirk, please confirm that there is no one in the room with you at the moment.'

'You and I are alone here, Alice.'

'As I'm to be found anywhere where there's an infopool terminal, I can accept your joke as a confirmation. I have a recording without a date and without any code. I have no idea how it got into the pool, but the address is definitely correct.'

'Shoot!'

It was Andrew's voice.

'Hello, Pete. If this is the first message you've received from me since that evening in Batticaloa, I'm sure you won't be able to make head or tail out of it. I have been informed that – how shall I put it – my original – in other words, I was killed in an accident. You must think this message is coming to you from the hereafter. A copy of me is talking to you at the moment. I'm now somewhere in Africa. They won't say where, but I've found out in the meantime that we're located in Angola. By we, I mean copies of Omero Pazzi, Cyril Wordsworth, Frank Nealon, Manfred Donsdorf and myself. Except for me, they're all laser specialists. We're on contract here to copy an armour-piercing neodymium laser cannon like the one the US army owns, but we don't have sufficient data at our disposal. We can't continue without the help of a mainframe computer. That's why they bought me, so I can establish the necessary contacts via infopool. Naturally, I'm being shadowed, but the security guards are easy to fool if you've got the computer on your side. We're all very bad copies with life expectancies of, at the most, a few weeks. My lower legs have been amputated. Probably to prevent me from running away. I can't sleep nights because of the pain and the medical care is terrible. Listen, Pete! There could be other copies of me. They probably weren't told that my original doesn't exist anymore. Keep a record of this and all other messages for me in chronological order on retrieval in a demand file and deposit a second set of these messages into my mailbox so that each copy of me can inform himself about what's going on and can reconstruct a biography if necessary. Send another set of these messages to Kenneth Buchan, Head of National Security. Tell him to keep all the information that runs through the infopool on call for me. Tell him I'd always suspected something, but never to this extent! I've no idea who could be carrying on the project and Roughtrade's business. Be careful, Peter, wherever you are. This kind of slave trade means big money. There could be hooks in the pool that spear certain names or codes that could draw attention to you. Be careful! Best regards, Andrew – End and out!'

I'm a devout Buddhist, Mr Kirk. I believe in rebirth, but whatever this is, it's something unnatural, something wicked and evil.

'Anything else, Alice?'

'Yes, Mr Kirk. A garbled message that was cut off after seven sentences. It was received about two and a half hours ago.'

It was Andrew's voice again. 'Hello, Peter. I won't be able to explain this to you in a few words, but, believe me, I'm not really Andrew. I've tried without success to reach Andrew. Tell him that someone's carrying on Roughtrade's business. He knows what he has to do. Tell him that I'm being forced to carry on the work I did on the MIDAS project. Tell him that Torre and Rodestrom are here. Tell him that I've been maimed and . . .'

Had they succeeded after all, even though Buchan denied it was possible. A sort of electronic Eucharist? A computerised tabernacle in which electric impulses are transformed into flesh and blood?

'The message is without sender and code. However it carries an infopool computer note. This message was entered at 1.23 p.m. local time via the local exchange network in Abu Dhabi.'

'Is the voice definitely Andrew Baldenham's?'

'It corresponds to the stored digital voice profile of Mr Andrew Baldenham. However, both messages do not have the alternating text code for analysing voice profiles that had been agreed upon. In spite of this, they were accepted by the computer as they contained a top priority secret code.'

'Anything else?'

'No, Mr Kirk.'

'Then I'd like you to keep both messages on retrieval for Mr Baldenham. Please add this postscript: Dear Andrew, Here are two messages from two other copies. Have spoken to Buchan. Happy 2017! Whatever computer you've got yourself into or wherever you are – I'll get you out. Best regards, Pete. End – And Alice, please send a copy of both messages for use outside the infopool with a postscript as follows: Mr Buchan,

Andrew once asked me if I believed in the resurrection of the flesh. I answered that I couldn't accept such a form of comfort. I've changed my mind. Rumpelstiltskin is my name, but luckily nobody knows it! You haven't told me the whole truth, Mr Buchan. Please call me back. End.'

Alice released an infochip with a quiet purr, which I stuck into the terminal of the NASA network. The scanner licked the electronic information from the plastic card and spat it back into my hand.

9

Solar Birds

Even if most astronauts do not admit it – a cold black stone of fear sits in the cage of our breasts while our eyes are fixed to the screen or wander restlessly over the instrument panels. There is always the fear that after a smooth and flawless countdown and with all systems GO, suddenly and without any previous warning, a large puff of black smoke will emerge from a hairline crack in the joint to one of the booster rockets and, in a matter of seconds, sweep you into darkness. This fear weighs on your soul and body during the first few minutes of ascent until the majestic storm of fire ebbs away, scattering its ashes to the four winds, and the burnt out rockets are ejected. Psychologists will call it the 'Challenger Syndrome', and any sort of conditioning against it has proven futile so far. That clear cold Tuesday afternoon in January more than thirty years ago witnessed the greatest emotional trauma ever to burden the American space program.

This explains the euphoric feeling when orbit has at last been reached. It helps to conquer that plunging sensation which invariably overcomes you.

I heaved a sigh of relief. I was in orbit at last. But I would only be able to relax when I was out in space. I never liked the cramped closeness of orbit life, was never completely free of agrophobia, although the doctor's sensors never gave me away. The Earth had an ominous effect on me – the overpowering nearness of its immense globe. I felt its brute force, although sometimes I wasn't conscious of its immediate presence. Even if common sense told me, 'you're not going to crash into it – you're circling around it,' I still couldn't get rid of that sultry animal fear of falling. A fear that could not be fooled by logic, a fear that chattered and shrieked until your eye found apparent strength in the sight of the station or one of the overhanging platforms nearby. These offered the necessary harmony – the longed-for point of reference where safety was found at last against all reason.

It's different in geostationary orbit; the Earth has moved to an objective distance. Although it's still very powerful, we aren't poised helplessly over it. It hovers in front of us, a celestial body, weightless, calmly kept in view or ignored.

The shuttle docked onto the Columbus. Two Sunbird mechanics, a com-technician and I were transferred to an OTV, an unrigged Hermes shuttle that would certainly never have survived another re-entry manoeuvre. The pilot hung over the entry, his emaciated legs hooked into a series of safety harnesses on the wall. I knew him. His name was Giulio Maspero. He hadn't been back to Earth for years as he had advanced atrophy of his leg muscles – a wheel chair case. He was wearing a black low-pressure overall and black suction socks. A tattered oxygen mask was hanging from his neck. He stowed the luggage away without saying a word and directed us to our seats. His strong arms and large hands made him look like a fiddler crab. In order to protect his body from bone fractures, he had sprayed the cockpit with thick black foam – a contourless velvet with the instrument panels twinkling in the background. The landing approach displayed a stellar cluster, a funnel made of tiny green square gates that got smaller and smaller in perspective – the flight lane of the Orbit

Transfer Vehicle through the material cloud of the construction site. The ESO shuttle took off, whirling on its three axles and, when it was out of the safety zone of the station, held its exact position for a two-minute slow-forward thrust. Most of us used the ten-hour flight to sleep or turned on our screens to one of the satellite stations. I stared at the instrument panels. The digital displays flickered over the edge of the screen. The gates in the flight lane moved here and there like tentacles. The computer searched for a path through the numerous hauler devices. Computer-controlled, they were responsible for transporting material to the construction site.

'Weren't you on Baldenham's team?' Maspero asked. He was sitting to the left of me in the pilot's seat. His pale swollen face and large white hands contrasted sharply with the black foam material. He stuffed his thin legs under him as if they were in the way.

'Yes.'

'I heard he was killed in a stupid accident.'

'Yes, a hotel fire.' I hesitated.

He turned halfway in my direction and I could feel him sizing me up out of the corner of his eye.

'Have you noticed how many scientists and technicians have been involved in strange accidents over the past few years?' he asked in a low voice. 'Most of them top specialists in their fields.'

'I've heard of a few strange cases.'

'Have you also heard of those mysterious doubles who suddenly appear from out of the blue? Bengt Rodestrom, Giuseppe Torre?'

'Yeah, some guys maintain they're . . . '

He shook his head. 'They're not impostors, if that's what you mean . . . ' He glanced back to make sure the other passengers weren't listening, then bent over to me and said quietly, 'Have you heard of Alonso Forli?'

'No.'

116

'An excellent pilot and a well-known journalist in Italy. We flew a lot together, South Pole and such. I had a talk with him four months ago in Milan. "You'll never believe me, Giulio," he said, "But there are real clones, exact replicas of people. I can even prove it." I didn't take him seriously at the time.' Maspero rubbed the back of his hand over his nose and snorted. 'Two weeks later, he was dead.'

He shrugged his shoulders. 'A hell of a funny story. You've got to see this one.' Without saying any more, he pointed to my com-line. A recording appeared on the screen to the left of my armrest. I pressed the earphones to my ears and turned them on. The announcer said: '. . . a Diwit Skylark plane has been missing since yesterday over the Western Sahara. The plane lost radio contact almost ninety minutes after the start in Djamena at 13.50 Central European Time. Two well-known Italian TV journalists, Alonso Forli and Pietro Barga, were on board. According to the RAI, they had met in a secret place in Chad to interview a man who maintained that he was Omero Pazzi, one of the top researchers in Laser Technology at Massachusetts Institute of Technology. The programme, which promised to be the sensation of the evening on Italian television, had to be cancelled. Search for the plane, which presumably crashed in the borderland between Chad and Libya, was resumed early in the morning. The RAI as well as the MIT have refused to comment on the incident so far. Also, from Omero Pazzi, who has not appeared in public for years, no reaction was . . . ' The shuttle pilot turned the video off. 'The wreckage was discovered later,' he said. 'Three people were found on board: Forli, Barga and Pazzi. "Mechanical breakdown" was the official reason. What a lot of bull shit! Not on a Diwit Skylark that Alonso always serviced himself. They must have hidden a bomb in his luggage or brought it down with a ground-to-air rocket.'

'I never heard anything about that accident,' I said. 'Andrew and I were in India at the time. Nanguneri, the antenna station . . . '

'Not so loud!' he said and glanced behind him. 'Were you with him when it happened?' He turned around to face me. 'Tell me all about it, Kirk!'

'There's nothing much to tell,' I protested, sorry I had said anything at all. 'It was a stupid hotel fire, that's all.'

'No peculiar circumstances?'

'What do you mean?'

'Army headquarters nearby, research institutes, hospitals – come on, Kirk! I don't believe you. I've been following such cases since Alonso's death. Plenty of time for research in between orbits. Baldenham fits into the picture perfectly. One of the best computer programmers! The Third World would pay a hell of a lot for him. But why did they kill him? Did he smell a rat?'

'Buchan said that the accident had already happened.'

'Had already happened?'

'Before the fire.'

Maspero nodded. 'Buchan?' he asked. 'Do you mean Kenneth Buchan, Head of National Security? What in hell's name has NASA got to do with this head-hunting game?'

'I've no idea. One thing is sure though. Buchan knows more than he's willing to say. You should really have a talk with him and tell him about your suspicions.'

Maspero looked at me warily, then he shook his head, grinning and, with a glance at the other passengers, whispered, 'Alonso told me that the RAI would have paid him a million dollars for the Pazzi story.'

'Well, he's got enough time now to think about how he could've spent it!'

Maspero shrugged his shoulders.

'Anyway, don't be astonished if one of these days you get a surprise call from Andrew Baldenham,' he said.

'You won't believe it, Maspero, but I've had several calls from him already. Two of them only yesterday.'

The pilot nodded. He wasn't the least bit surprised. 'I knew he'd be in great demand.'

Sunbird 4 resembled a huge web in which thousands of fireflies had become entangled while, from afar, the unfinished solar network looked like an immense, tattered lace cloth. The eight housing modules moved closer together with solar cell paddles, hauling devices, docking trunks and softly glittering gold observation areas like giant, surrealistic beetles in formation. Maspero guided the shuttle to the docking trunk of a housing module – a converted booster rocket. The upper part contained the observatory stations and the lounge. The middle part had been converted into living and sleeping quarters and the stern held the bale-out exit. 'Tins' it was called by the orbit crew. There was a crowded closeness everywhere. Each section had its own unmistakable smell. I waved to Maspero, took one last deep breath, climbed on board, stowed James away in the stern and put my belongings into my berth. My nameplate was still on the door as the accommodation had been flown in from Sunbird 3. My glance automatically wandered to the next berth. The name of Andrew Baldenham had disappeared.

The feeling that I was home again vanished. I called up my work schedule on the screen and studied it. Brian Ferguson, the project boss, suddenly tuned in and said, 'Welcome on board, Kirk.' He had that hunted look of an engineer who has to repair two technical failures at once. He disappeared from the screen immediately. According to the schedule, I was to start work in less than seven hours. I tried to get some sleep, but wasn't very successful. It would take me a while to get used to the noises that constantly kept me awake in the metal cylinder surroundings: the gurgling of liquids, the hissing of air, the chirping and whining of power engines and pumps, the rumbling of the bulkheads and floodgates, the whispering and fluttering of the life supporting systems.

Buchan was right about one thing: it certainly took my mind off Andrew. In fact, I hardly had time to think at all. Work in orbit is hard and full of privations. EFOS is not a non-profit organisation, but a full-fledged corporation with NASA as partner. Capital investment in the project is high. Material transport to the perigee is expensive, not to mention the exorbitant costs of human transport, let alone feeding and caring for the crew. The standards are extremely high as a result. The impossible is demanded of everyone and the losses are correspondingly high.

I often fell asleep over a meal or while watching a film. In spite of this, I climbed into the com-cabin after every shift and called Alice up on the screen. There was nothing in the mailbox but advertisements, greetings from friends, bills and statements from insurance companies or banks. Ruth seemed to have forgotten me. No other messages from Andrew and still no reaction from Buchan.

The solar network was shaping up into its final form; the power station had been manoeuvred into position and nestled into place like a spider. The antennas, pointed in the direction of the earth, carried out their first test runs between Swakopmund and Port-au-Prince, Montevideo and Nouakchott.

It was on the 14th of February, a Tuesday, about an hour after the end of my shift. I was spooning in one of those pasty looking meals, which, if the name said anything, consisted of turkey, rice and mixed vegetables and which had been embedded in some kind of gluey substance to make it edible in a weightless atmosphere.

In between mouthfuls, I squirted some coffee into my mouth from a plastic bottle. I was watching the news on the monitor on the wall, when suddenly Mabel Hertz, a telemetry colleague who was on shift in the com-center, interrupted the programme. She shook back her black curls to reveal a small pale face. She said with a cheerful smile, 'Peter, you're wanted in the com-center immediately.'

'Who is it?' I asked in surprise, and looked at the diagonal belt over her breast that strapped her into her seat. She had on a black T-shirt with a peacock embroidered on it, with tiny coloured metal sequins arranged in exciting patterns.

'Alice from infopool says there's a video-recording for you. And ground control is trying to fix up a good connection from the Cape. If I understand rightly, the big chief of security himself wants to talk to you,' she said. Her slim, somewhat boney finger was poised over the off button. She laughed a flirtatious laugh and was obviously enjoying my reaction.

'I . . . I'll be right with you,' I assured her hastily, and squeezed the empty tin foil package into the waste cutter at the head of the table.

The picture on the screen was the very one that had haunted me day and night – Andrew in a wheel-chair.

'I think I'm going mad!' I whispered.

'I received your message, Pete, and succeeded in getting into my mailbox in order to study my turbulent past. Thanks for putting it together for me.'

He raised his hand weakly. 'I've managed at long last to produce a visual display.' He was overcome by a fit of coughing. He continued breathing heavily. 'It looks bad. Nealon and Donsdorf are dead; Wordsworth is dying and I haven't seen Pazzi for days.' The camera swung across laboratory equipment and zoomed in on a face, the face of a white man with a closely-cropped white beard. Blood had dried black at the corner of his mouth. His cheeks, forehead and nose were covered with flies. I didn't know who the man was. The camera wandered on – more dead, mainly blacks, some in laboratory coats, the rest soldiers in uniform. Bloated bodies slashed to pieces. Flies everywhere.

'It happened sooner than we expected.' The camera swung back to Andrew. An emaciated hand held onto one wheel of his chair, while the other activated the remote control of the camera.

'The South Africans have been using some kind of infernal biological concoction. The rats are even kicking the bucket. It doesn't seem to have any effect at all on the flies, though. I got through to Buchan. He confirmed my suspicions. Can't tell you anymore.' He bent forward and breathed heavily. It took him all his willpower to sit up and whisper, 'Farewell, Pete. Hope you're safe.'

'Andrew!' I called before it dawned on me that it was a recording.

Andrew's picture disappeared from the screen.

'Farewell,' I said softly.

Alice appeared as friendly and good-humoured as ever.

'The transmission line to Cape Canaveral still has a few minutes left, so I'll keep you company, Mr Kirk. As you've forbidden advertising spots, shall I run a couple of cartoons for you instead?'

'Thank you, Alice, I'm not in the mood for cartoons.'

'Sorry, Mr Kirk. Would you like anything else?'

'No, thank you.'

'I need a power of attorney from you, Pete,' Buchan blustered his way onto the screen and looked at me angrily. He was sitting at his desk with his shirt unbuttoned at the collar and stabbed his finger threateningly in the direction of the camera. 'I need your signature to be able to get into your infopool mailbox if necessary.'

'Why?'

'I want to be able to take immediate action in case some information turns up in your mailbox on the Baldenham affair.'

'But I've had every call transferred to you that . . . '

'I said *"immediate action"*, Kirk.'

'I don't like people prying into my private affairs . . . '

He laughed sarcastically. 'My God! Don't be so prudish! What are you trying to hide? Your lousy marriage?' I looked at him annoyed.

'Okay! I didn't mean it. Listen, Pete, I want to keep you out of this. You've just seen the video from Angola. They're after more than you can imagine.'

'I imagine what they're after.'

'How?'

'I just imagine, that's all!'

He looked at me critically and finally dismissed the subject with a wave of his hand. 'Be reasonable, Pete! I'm responsible for your security and the security of many others. I'm talking about your neck, man! There won't be that many calls from Andrew anymore. The interval from the date of the recording has become so great in the meantime that each copy will check his own mailbox to see whether or not a former copy has left a message or has attempted to set up a biography.'

'A copy, sir?'

He was furious and knocked angrily with his knuckles on the desk. 'You think you're really smart, eh?' Suddenly, he grinned and said in a conciliatory tone. 'Believe me, Pete. The less you know, the better it is for you!'

'Rumpelstiltskin is my name, but luckily nobody knows it . . . '

'I want your signature, Kirk!' he thundered at me.

I shook my head. 'Brew today, tomorrow bake, after that the child I'll take.'

'May the devil get you – you joker!' He screamed and cut the connection.

I grinned into the empty screen, slightly dazed, and was surprised at my own stubbornness. I didn't like the idiot because he had succeeded in letting me feel his authority. His remarks about my marriage hadn't hurt me at all. The man had lost my respect.

'You stupid fool,' I said, and sniggered to myself in a fit of childish triumph.

'Do you need me anymore, Mr Kirk?' Alice asked.

'Probably more than ever, honey, but not at the moment.'

'Heh, are you going to spend the night here, Pete?' Mabel asked. The peacock glittered seductively.

'Can I count on you, baby?'

'Clear the com-room immediately! Or do you think you're the only infopool customer?'

In the end, Buchan was right. Almost. On March 6th, a Monday, Joseph Martinez, Dean Howard, Charles Cadigan and I had just finished inspecting the antenna and were on the point of being let in. We did this in pairs as the lock chamber at the stern of the housing modules was very cramped and, in pairs, it made it easier to help one another out of our spacesuits. Martinez and Howard went in first. Cadigan and I followed. Martinez had already disappeared through the bulkhead, while Howard dawdled in his red underwear and rubbed his head with a towel. His black face was gleaming with sweat.

Then Cadigan climbed into the inner gate. I followed close behind. I opened the lock on his helmet and he was just on the point of opening mine when I happened to glance at Howard's face. His mouth was open as he stared in speechless amazement at what must have been happening outside the lock. I turned around as quickly as I could in my space suit and, through the scratched plastic of the lock chamber window, saw a huge, tightly packed material bundle heading straight for us. Quick as lightning, I released my eraser that I always carried with me on my left wrist. The reverse driving mechanism of the hauler started to work at full speed. A white vapour wall of gas swelled up to form a hazy halo and exploded in a flurry of snow, but it was too late, of course. A second later, the housing module convulsed like the electrified muscle of an American bison torn out of its anchoring. A couple of cubic yards of poles crashed with a loud noise through the plastic stern into the changing room, splintering the window to pieces.

Both my feet were stuck in the safety harnesses provided, according to instructions. I was catapulted like a pendulum backwards until my helmet crashed against the wall. That was my luck. At least I was swept out of the path of the material bundle as it crashed, vehemently, not wanting to come to a stop.

Cadigan was not as lucky as I. Either he had pulled his feet out of the harnesses when he helped me to open my helmet or they were ripped off during the crash. At any rate, he was shot into the direction of the stern like a torpedo bomber. I reached out to grab him when he had reached my level and succeeded in catching and holding on to him tightly.

I couldn't see, thank God, what had happened to Howard. His scream was lost in the roar of the crash and something red splattered along the poles – impossible that it had once been a human body. The bulkhead to the passageway slammed shut and James began to lament in a loud computer voice, 'Close helmet! Rapid drop in pressure . . . ' At that very moment a heavy fog started forming above me, streaming out of the leak. Shouts could be heard over the construction site loudspeakers. Voices drowned one another out with shrill instructions and garbled commands until Ferguson, bellowing at the top of his voice, worked his way through to the front. 'Quiet on all channels! This is an emergency. Rescue teams to module 4. Stop all material movement in sector 1! I repeat – this is an emergency! Rescue team to module 4! Stop all material movement in sector 1. Who, in hell's name, is responsible for this God damn mess? Calling central unit – I need a detailed computer record of this – IMMEDIATELY! Whoever's responsible for this bungling mess, I'll kick out of the lock personally.'

Either the hauler's engine had not been damaged by the crash, or it was due to the elasticity of the module's walls – at any rate, the bent poles began to pull back with an agonising slowness, shrieking and grating in the process. The air was pulled out, too. A siren began to whine excitedly, the noise becoming gradually thinner as if it were moving away. In the walls, four jets started blowing simultaneously, spitting light blue, sticky, self-hardening foam into the airstream that was propelled to the leak. But when it arrived at the hole that had been torn by the rods, the automatic seal naturally didn't work – the foam fizzled out ineffectively into space.

My helmet lock was open. In order to close it again, I would have had to let go of Cadigan. I was still clutching him with both arms. I prayed that the harnesses holding my feet would not give out under the double burden, as the escaping air tried to drive us out through the hole with the force of a tornado. It was as if a team of buffalos were trying to take off my boots. My knees and hip joints snapped in pain. The nervously wailing siren above our heads seemed to be miles away and James persevered: 'Close helmet! Rapid fall in pressure . . . ' I cursed the idiotic spacesuit computer, but couldn't comply.

Cadigan was in a worse state than I. His helmet had been half open when it happened; he was losing air faster than I and was no longer conscious. I could hear a blubbering hiss as air was pulled out of his lungs. The top of his helmet was filling up with a reddish coloured foam. I was glad that I couldn't see his face. My arms were tightly around his bloating body and I could feel his bowels emptying into his suit.

I remembered a video that had been shown to would-be astronauts in the first stages of our training in order to illustrate the dangers involved in a sudden decompression phase. They used a white mouse in a glass cell. The small, curious animal that nervously snuffled and pattered around turned into a rose-coloured ball, the size of a football, and, a split second later, was nothing but red fog with drops of blood and particles of fur speckling the glass.

Hopefully, it wouldn't happen that fast. Cadigan on the other hand . . . Suddenly, I heard a loud crack and felt excruciating pain. Fire pokers seemed to be piercing my ears and my head felt as if it were being torn apart. All I could hear was the static roar of my own brain. My ears felt as if they were stuck inside my skull.

The storm was over. The worst was to come. I was holding Cadigan tightly like a cop holding on to his booty. He was swelling up in my arms like a balloon filling up with air. My gloves were hooked, one into the other, like mechanical gripping devices. My hands were cold and numb. You can let go of him now I said to myself. He won't be torn away anymore. But I was incapable of loosening a muscle. I wondered furiously where the rescue team was and, at the same time, I knew with unusual mental clarity that only three, at the most four minutes had passed since the accident.

My breathing slowed down considerably although James continued hurling his entire reserve of air into my helmet. But the reserves were limited. I grit my teeth together, but couldn't prevent phlegm and bile from finding a way out. In spite of trying to control my reflexes, I had to spit out. I blew through my nose with all my might, according to instructions, in order not to choke on my own stomach contents or a haemorrhage. Sun-spots clouded my retina, a whirl of colours – cinnabar, emerald and violet. The spots developed into galaxies and blocked my field of vision completely, intertwining and devouring one another and plunging into darkness. Agonising pain consumed me from my ears, right through to the innermost reaches of my skull. My temples throbbed and hammered from behind against my eyes, as if trying to force them out of their sockets. My lids were ice, my tear fluid had evaporated. My face became a glacier. Darkness descended.

The colourful galaxies disintegrated into prostellar ashes, clouds of dust, light years away, in which musty red new centres of gravity glowed. Dark cinders were floating across my field of vision. They changed their course with the speed of lightning when I moved my eyelids, drifted towards me, only to jerk back convulsively until they dissolved into huge boulders and disappeared. In the distance, solitary pulsars blinked. Once again, debris slipped out of the corners of my eyes, slipped in once again in the form of sharp-edged pieces of coke, came to a standstill and slid back out, chafing painfully.

'Is he dead, doctor?'

The voice was far off in the distance – Ferguson himself. I wanted to open my eyes but, at that very moment, a swell of lava splashed towards me.

'He was unbelievably lucky. In spite of the fact that his helmet was open, decompression was not sudden. The emergency air pack in his helmet tried to compensate. Naturally, it was depleted in less than five minutes.'

So you fought for my life then, James. I love you, you old skunk.

'And Cadigan?'

'If Kirk had not held on to him, he'd be dead. It would've been the end of him if we'd have had to look for him in space. He's in a coma, but he'll survive. His hearing has been completely destroyed and he'll need an eye transplant, but his optic nerves have remained intact. They'll be able to restore part of his eyesight and certainly part of his hearing. But I can't tell you anything definite as I don't have the equipment.'

'Transportable?'

'Both of them?'

'Wednesday?'

'Not before Saturday.'

'Okay, I'll see to it that the necessary steps are taken.'

'And Howard?'

'Sir . . . I'm sorry, sir. We couldn't rescue all that much of him. He was hit practically naked . . . Do they know . . . ?'

'Yes, but I want to wait for the results of the report.'

'I understand, sir.'

I could feel the sting of the injection needle. The galaxies of ashes began spinning again, but I slowly lost track of them as the injection took hold.

'Kirk?' Someone was patting my naked cheek. The bandages had obviously been removed. 'Can you hear me?'

All I could see was a landscape of grey streaks and murky pools vaguely resembling a human face – Dr Lemberg's face.

'Yes,' I croaked. My throat felt as if clammy rusty iron had been stored there for centuries. I tried to nod, but wasn't able to. Something cool filled my mouth. It tasted as bitter as camphor and as fresh as mint. I swallowed and began to cough, but at least it helped me breathe more freely.

Ferguson was bending over me. He looked exhausted and haggard from lack of sleep.

'You probably want to ask how such a thing could happen. Go on – ask me! I've been asked the same question a million times in the past forty-eight hours. I can tell you exactly what happened. Someone was tampering with the assembly program, erased the date of certain automatic safety programs. It's not that easy. Only a top computer specialist is capable of such tricks. Do you know Herb Ashley?'

'No.' My voice sounded very strange.

'New up here. He was sent up to replace Baldenham who was bumped off by those bums.'

'Sir, that's not what happened. Baldenham was not . . . '

'What?' His blood-shot eyes sent out a look of reproval as if I'd been caught trying to blow my nose into the American flag.

'I was there when it happened, sir. He wasn't . . . ' I stopped completely exhausted.

'Don't be so naive! Of course, he was killed by those bastards! In Sri Lanka, I believe. They probably wanted to kidnap him and he resisted. It isn't the first time this has happened either. They need our scientists because the silly fools are not capable of anything at all. I'd cut off the scoundrels' energy for a few weeks, then we'd see how many of them would survive. They'd be in the trees in no time again. Wanna bet?'

'If you say so, sir.'

He was the type of person who would not listen to reason, one of those super efficient types – often found in technicians, engineers or even scientists – who never have time to think because they are so busy being efficient. They're thankful for every preconceived idea they can assume, even if the ideas are in blatant contrast to their profession. I'd seen it often enough. 'How reliable you technicians are in contrast,' Buchan had once said.

'Ashley was supposed to be on surveillance only. He

was in training. Starts fooling around with the program – the silly fool. Maintains he lost control and panicked. Filthy lies! Starts moving half a ton of antenna poles in the direction of the housing modules just at the very moment that you happen to be entering the lock.'

'What are you trying to say?' I croaked.

'He wanted to run those poles right through you.'

'But there were four of us – Martinez, Howard, Cadigan and . . .'

He wouldn't let me finish. 'He wanted you, Kirk!'

'Who says that? What does he say . . . ?' I could hardly speak. I felt a pain in my chest.

'We won't be able to ask him. He went through the lock before I could question him – without his space-suit.'

'My God!'

'Some say that maybe it really was an accident and that he acted out of remorse – but as far as I'm concerned it's quite obvious, he wanted you!'

'Where do you get that idea?' I asked, breathing heavily. I tried to sit up. The doctor laid his hand on my chest and stopped me.

Ferguson looked at me for a moment, lost in pensive thought. He looked very old and tired. Then he put both hands on his cheeks and brushed his fingertips over his eyes and forehead, tousling his already dis-heveled grey hair. He looked like some kind of sullen bird caught mating.

'Listen, Kirk! I don't know what's going on here, but security down at the Cape are of the same opinion and they also find my theory plausible and logical. Buchan nodded furiously when I reported the incident to him, as if he expected it to happen. He ordered us to look for Ashley's body and send it down for an autopsy. Do you know why? He wouldn't tell me. As if there'd be anything left to perform an autopsy on with his innards all hanging out!' He shrugged his shoulders in resignation. 'Had to stop all work on the construction site for the past forty-eight hours. I have thirty men outside trying to find that lousy body – or, to be more precise, what's left of it! And that here in this junkyard of a stationary orbit, where you could hide a shuttle. The body could have drifted umpteen miles away. Autopsy! Pure waste of time and fuel!'

The doctor, who hovered on the other side of my bed, nodded zealously in agreement.

'I don't need to tell you how difficult it is to keep the building material together. And it will take us days to work out a new hauling program – on condition they send us a top software specialist up with the next shuttle. This stupid bungle has cost us a whole week!'

Ferguson jolted the suspension over my bed in his anger. The pieces of cinder started seesawing rhythmically before my closed eyes. I lifted my eyelids nervously.

'Be careful, sir!' the doctor said.

'Excuse me,' Ferguson grumbled and my optical cosmos found rest once again.

'Buchan wants you down there as soon as possible, Kirk. With the Wednesday shuttle, if the doctor gives his okay.'

'Medically speaking, I have no objections, sir.'

'I'll be glad to get rid of you, Kirk. There's one thing I can't have up here and that's trouble. I've got a schedule to follow. I'm expected to finish in time – no matter what happens. this project means a hell of a lot of money!'

'Yes, sir.' I replied.

Sixteen hours later, I was down at Columbus Station. I was carefully pushed through the docking tunnel and strapped to a pressure bed at the back. Strange faces floated by. My eyes were running with tears. The pilot patted me on my cheek.

'Don't cry, little boy. You're going home to Mummy,' he said grinning.

'You're breaking my heart!' I croaked.

Black plastic bags filled with the deep-frozen rests of Herb Ashley and Dean Howard were hanging in the cargo space behind us. Had the poles hit a second later, Cadigan and I would be hanging there now, I thought to myself. They would have hit us naked. My stomach was so queasy I had trouble holding it down. It wasn't due to the braking manoeuvre as the shuttle entered, either.

A hell of a close call!

10

Hi-Tech Shares Close Higher

'That was close, Kirk,' Kenneth Buchan said, stomping back and forth between his desk and the window. 'Damn close,' he repeated ominously. He was wearing a dark pin-striped suit with a waistcoat, a white shirt and a silver-grey tie. He looked as if he had just been invited to a dinner party at the White House. In my shabby leather jacket and my old corduroy jeans, I could sense his reproach and kept my eyes on my well-worn running shoes.

'Have you got something against me?' he asked suddenly.

I looked up in surprise. 'No, Sir, why should I?'

He nodded and looked impatiently at the terminal on his wrist. 'I had you brought directly here from the hospital,' he said, rocking back and forth in his elegant patent leather shoes, 'to eliminate all possible risks.'

Since my return to earth, I realised I was being constantly followed by middle-aged men who tried to be inconspicuous, but stuck out like sore thumbs. They usually carried a trenchcoat over one arm and, if it was raining, they were sure to be wearing their trenchcoats and still carrying one over their arms. In the hospital during the week spent recovering, one of them had been constantly posted in front of my door.

'This affair has been blown up out of all proportion. I can no longer take responsibility for it alone.'

'You mean as far as Andrew Baldenham is concerned?'

He hesitated. 'Yes, among others.'

'Has anyone heard from him in the meantime?'

'Yes,' he said, hesitating even more. 'He's contacted me several times now.'

'Have other copies surfaced?'

He nodded vaguely.

His terminal began to blink. He raised it to his ear. 'Yes . . . yes, Sir . . . Okay . . . I'll bring him over right away!'

'Let's go!' he said, turning in my direction, and opened the door. Quick as a weasel, he slithered past me down the corridor and opened the door to a small conference room. 'Please come in,' he said to me and nodded encouragingly.

I saw two men on the other side of the room. One was standing at a table and rewinding a pocket recorder. The other was sitting on one of the chairs informally scattered about the room. He stood up when we entered.

'Mr Ashkenside of the CIA,' Buchan introduced the man at the table. He was short and neatly dressed in an inconspicuous brown suit. He turned his thin, expressionless face towards me. His dark eyes peered through his gold-rimmed glasses that were so thick they looked as if they were made of bullet-proof glass. Could this snooping rodent be the boss?

'McEnroe of the CIA,' Buchan said. The man who had stood up as we entered shook hands with me spontaneously. He was a hefty, stockily-built man with an imposing stomach that hung over his belt, which had slipped down to make room for it. His plaid jacket was hopelessly wrinkled. He nodded to me with a wry look and said, 'Frank's my name. Pleased to meet ya, Pete.' He was definitely the Great Dane, the retriever.

'This is Peter Kirk,' Buchan explained unnecessarily as surely both of them knew more about my past than I did.

135

'Sit down, Pete,' Frank McEnroe said and pointed to the chairs.

'I'd rather stand.'

'As you like, but it'll take awhile.' He yanked his pants up and sat down with a thud onto one of the chairs. I sat down. He examined me, his brow furrowed in anger. He pursed his protruding lips to a reproachful pout. As I had no idea what I could have done, I presumed that this was his on-duty face.

The short, wiry man continued playing around with the recorder. He stared at the machine, his face deadly serious, and touched the sensor button with his thin forefinger. He had dark, closely cropped, curly hair and a thin moustache just under his nose. Ashkenside? He'd probably Americanised his name. Was he Armenian? His eyes were close together, typical of the incorruptible bureaucrat – correct, absolutely logical, pitiless and uncompromising. A man who would ruthlessly work his way to the top in any Secret Service the world over. Be careful! I said to myself. He's a two-legged computer. A monster, who secretly slurps oysters and holds a string of magnificent prostitutes.

As if he had read my thoughts, he raised his head with a sniff and looked at me. I felt very ill at ease.

Buchan, who had taken up position beside him, suddenly folded his arms in front of his chest and bristled with his own importance.

'Mr Kirk,' he began formally, obviously trying to impress me. 'You've put us in a very difficult position.'

'How's that?' I asked defiantly.

'Why didn't you tell us, you comedian,' he blustered away, 'that you visited Fred Kissinger in New York.'

'Why should you be interested in that?'

Buchan looked at the other two imploringly as if to say, 'See for yourselves. It's not my fault! He's a pigheaded madman.' 'Because it's a miracle you're still alive!' he screamed.

McEnroe raised his hand to stop the racket and made a few silencing noises with his lips.

'Just how much does Mr Kirk know?' Ashkenside inquired in a low voice.

I had never seen Buchan so zealous. 'Mr Baldenham seems to have given him . . . ah . . . access to some information. God knows what his reasons were. It would exceed my sphere of competence if I . . .' Ashkenside cut him short with an almost imperceptible nod of his head.

Coward, I thought to myself.

'Then you just listen to this, Mr Kirk,' Ashkenside said, and tapped the sensor button on the recorder.

An unknown male voice said angrily. 'What do we care what those brown apes do to them. Since when are you so squeamish? They're willing to pay a fortune for replicants of that bird. Every one of those top officers would have loved to fuck her.'

'But they killed her!'

It was Kissinger's voice! 'Oh, my God! Given the quality of the copies they make, it really doesn't matter whether they die a few hours earlier or later. You were never this sensitive, Kiss?'

'No names!' Kissinger hissed in anger.

'Nonsense! This is a safe line.'

'Listen! Nancy Tanner is not just anyone. Every errand boy, every taxi driver in Colombo knows her. Someone's sure to notice and there'll be hell to pay. They should keep the replicants in the officers' quarters under lock and key, as agreed. Instead I hear that those idiots are letting themselves be seen in broad daylight with them.'

'I'll check into that, sir.'

'Yes, do! You can't imagine how shocked I was when that guy suddenly turned up with a letter from her. Thank God it was not a letter from a replicant, but a very old letter from the real Nancy. But this could happen every day!'

'Did you get the impression that Kirk fellow wanted to sound us out?'

'No, I didn't. He didn't ask any questions. But, just the same, we shouldn't let him walk around freely.'

'He's from NASA.'

'So what?'

'Special security measures have been taken on the part of the space authorities.' Buchan looked at me and nodded. McEnroe was busy with his finger nails. Ashkenside stared indifferently straight in front of him and listened.

'Since when have security measures caused you any trouble?' Kissinger asked sarcastically. 'Besides, he's walking around here in New York all alone. He said he's staying at a friend's place.'

'Then he's lying. We've had two things on the hook today. The name Roughtrade was mentioned twice. Both times the receiver of the message was a certain Peter Kirk in Hotel Transfer near Washington Square.'

'And what are you going to do about it?'

'I sent two of my men over there right away, but the idiot had already flown.'

'Damn it all! Then you'll have to think of something else!'

Ashkenside touched a button with the tip of his finger and stopped the recording. Buchan hissed. 'I thought as much,' he said, 'and that's why I ordered you to come here right away and had you sent up into space. I thought you'd be safe up there. What a laugh! You nincompoop, if you had just told us . . . '

'This recording was made by the FBI,' Ashkenside interrupted in a low nasal voice. 'It was recorded during a routine investigation of unauthorised safe lines. During a search run, when the word NASA appeared, a copy was automatically sent to the security head-quarters of NASA on . . . ' he checked the documents in front of him, 'on the 2nd of January.' Good God, at that time I hadn't even started out into space!

'You can't imagine how much material like this comes in daily,' Buchan said, embittered. 'Unfortunately, NASA is not as well staffed as other comparable organisations.'

'I presume Mr Kirk has some questions to ask us,' Mr Ashkenside said. 'We'll answer them to the best of our knowledge after deciding, of course, whether his questions merit answering. Mr Kirk, I must do everything within my official power to make it quite clear to you that any information we might give you is top secret, and passing on any of this information will have legal consequences.'

I nodded. 'Just because the name of "Roughtrade" was mentioned? The guy doesn't interest me, although he seems to represent some kind of key figure. Anyway, he's been dead for more than twelve years now . . . ' McEnroe looked at me critically. 'Why does an alarm go off to certain people when his name goes through infopool?'

'Well, first of all, there's the technical side of it,' Ashkenside said. 'Such a word sensor only makes sense if the name is unusual and if it appears in a definite semantic area.'

'I don't mean that. I was told that this . . . this hook could only be inserted on strictest orders from top national or international security. How is it possible that Kissinger and his buddies, without fear of punishment, were able to put their hook in infopool in order to find out where I was staying and try to kill me?'

'That's the legal aspect,' Ashkenside said, 'which has puzzled us for a long time now. Infopool is a multi-national corporation that – aside from a few exceptions – cooperates with all the countries in the world. You can be sure, Mr Kirk, that . . . there are . . . ah . . . governments that are not our allies, who have to be granted rights of this kind.'

'I understand.'

'You also know, Mr Kirk,' Ashkenside continued, 'that these security measures apply to a procedure for producing copies of people.'

'MIDAS.'

'MIDAS was a secret government project that did research in that field. It was cancelled in the year 2003 when they had proof that the procedure was bound to fail.'

'And in spite of that, copies are being produced?'

Ashkenside had the annoying habit of never answering immediately. At first, he didn't react at all, seemed not to be listening as if waiting for an invisible interpreter to pose the question in another language. After ten or fifteen seconds, he raised his head and started to answer.

'Yes, but they're inadequate copies with a life expectancy of between several hours and a few weeks, depending on the quality of the recording and the duplicating run. The quality can, in principle, according to Horace Simonson's theory, not really be improved. It's a sort of uncertainty principle found in particle physics: a higher degree of accuracy can't be achieved because an improvement in the recording and reproduction quality automatically means a more powerful intervention into the molecular structure itself. According to this, there's an absolute limiting value. A higher degree of accuracy would reduce the quality and the result – mistakes in the molecular structure, i.e. more toxic and carcinogen connections would occur that could destroy the organism sooner or later. MIDAS was discontinued after that. The results of their research were put under lock and key and all information was blocked.'

'The information block was obviously not drastic enough.'

'Unfortunately, there was a leak.'

'Roughtrade?'

'Roughtrade. He got wind of the fact that his project would be cancelled and channeled out research documents in time, and perhaps even MIDAS recordings of his own equipment, to private individuals in order to continue his work.'

'But shortly after, he was . . . '

I stopped, taken aback at the thought.

Ashkenside nodded. 'We haven't been able to prove anything as his body was almost completely burned, but it's safe to assume that he probably substituted a copy of himself and that he's still living.'

'And carrying on his business.'

'A profit-making business, trading in hi-tech software,' McEnroe said grinning. 'Top scientists in every field, for every possible need, at connoisseur's prices. Canned eggheads for the power-hungry dictators of the Third World. Here, a mathematician, there, a computer specialist and even an atomic physicist. Have you noticed that the number of countries with atomic power has risen to over fifty during the past few years? Even such countries as Venezuela and Burkina-Faso. Roughtrade must've made an unbelievable fortune in the past ten years.'

'Motives such as revenge might have played a role at the beginning,' Ashkenside said. 'At first only copies of his antagonists surfaced.' Ashkenside's thick glasses gleamed. Had I seen the hint of a malicious smile steal to the corners of his mouth? So it wasn't a brocas areal disturbance, but an acquired lack of emotion. 'Wouldn't it be ironic,' he continued, 'if he only used them to finance his research. Later, his customers' demands ought to have been more precise and the possibility of blackmail certainly much greater.'

'But how did he get the people?'

'Just look at Andrew Baldenham, for example,' Buchan interjected.

'As a rule he met them at scientific conventions, preferably in cities like Manila, Nairobi, Rio de Janeiro, Colombo, New Delhi, but also in Montreal or Mexico City. The person was drugged in his hotel room and then taken to a suitable place where a recording could be made. They wake up again in their hotel beds, feeling slightly indisposed and worn out, but that is not unusual at such meetings, especially if the convention took place in cities where the climate and food are different.'

'But Andrew was mutilated and killed.'

'I don't believe he was killed, although it can't be completely ruled out. He, as a close colleague of Roughtrade, would have realised immediately what was going on. An accident obviously occurred. Probably power failure or faulty equipment during the scanning cycle. The laser beams could have burned his feet off during the breakdown. They staged the rest in order to cover up the incident, perhaps even went as far as to really kill him. Murder is very rare though – although lately there've been several cases of murder to make the replicas more submissive.'

'Herb Ashley,' Buchan added.

'Herb Ashley?' I asked. 'The computer specialist who was allegedly trying to kill me?'

'The autopsy proved that the man responsible for the accident on Sunbird 4 was a replicant.' Buchan shook his head. 'It's a mystery to me how he got through the medical examinations. We're going to have to tighten our controls drastically. The police have found the body of the original in the meantime.'

'Why was he killed?'

'If a person only exists as a recording, the copy could be

persuaded that medical stabilisation might be possible. In exchange, one can expect a . . . ah . . . favour.'

'Quite a sacrifice,' McEnroe inserted, and nodded to me.

'And what about Nancy Tanner?'

'Also active in self-sacrifice,' McEnroe laughed, 'albeit involuntarily.'

'Disgusting side-effects,' Ashkenside raised his hands in defence. 'They've nothing to do with our real problem.'

But McEnroe wasn't listening. He stood up and came over to me. 'Have you ever seen video nasties?' he asked me, rolling his eyes. 'Death and sex?'

'Yes,' I said. 'I remember vaguely.'

I remembered only too clearly that terrible videotape that was secretly passed around at college. *The Amorous Adventures of Monsieur A*, I think it was called. The hideous picture had haunted me in my nightmares for years. There was one scene I would never forget: a luxurious salon furnished in black and white. Two tall, handsome and slender men were in the room with masks and fantastic feathers on their heads, shoulders and hips as if Salvador Dali had designed the costumes for Mozart's *Magic Flute*. Their movements were those of dancers, but they had something arrogant about them – fascinating and at the same time repulsive – something inhuman, yes, something not of this earth. A young black girl, beautiful, almost a child, an immaculate body, naked except for a black and white feathered mask, dark shining skin – the camera work was excellent. While one of the bird beings copulated with her from behind, holding onto her hips, the upper part of her body bent horizontally forward, her small pointed breasts hanging down like the teats of a beautiful wild animal, her arms spread out as if in flight, her legs wrapped around the lower legs of the man, her mouth open as her pleasure culminated, the third figure raised a sword in one hand. It was splendidly adorned with rubies. With the other hand, he seized the head of the girl and severed it from her body with one stroke. The other, with solemn movements, continued to copulate with the torso as if nothing had happened, while the executioner bedded the severed head in a white porcelain bowl filled with red and white blossoms.

The camera paused showing the face of the girl, zoomed in for a close-up: the fantastic mask made of dove and raven feathers, the delicate, but somewhat broad nose, the mouth open as if in a scream. A never-ending tongue glided over the small chin and crept among the blossoms like an animal set free.

'In those days, they picked up inexperienced prostitutes from the street,' McEnroe said. 'Promised them five hundred dollars for a few shots in a sex film. We used to find their bodies in the basements of abandoned houses in the Bronx. Some of them were so badly mutilated, we couldn't have them identified. I was a young policeman at the time. I tell ya, I'll never forget those scenes of horror.' He glared at me in anger as if he suspected me of complicity. 'I swear, if I'd have caught the guys responsible, I'd have castrated them all with my Magnum 41!'

Buchan stood with his shoulders hunched and seemed somewhat pained at the thought. Bored, Ashkenside examined the metal grating up on the ceiling. The shadowy blades of a fan were moving noiselessly behind it.

'Then the FBI decided to take rigorous action,' McEnroe continued with satisfaction, 'and the obscenities stopped from one day to the next – with the result that they then took to shooting their films in Brazil or the border-land between Peru and Ecuador, choosing their women to be mutilated from the Amazon Indians. All they had to promise was some grub, the perverted pigs!' He folded his fleshy hands on his stomach, sprawled his fingers and shoved his thumbs into his waistband. 'However, what happened there was no longer under our jurisdiction.'

'And what's that got to do with Nancy Tanner?' I asked.

'That's the latest variant,' he said and shrugged his shoulders, 'and you can't catch them on legal grounds. Officially, replicants don't exist.'

'Are you trying to tell me that . . . that Nancy Tanner is being copied over and over again and . . . ?'

'Jesus, you're slow in the uptake,' he said and stretched his chin out in anger. He made a fist with his right hand and punched his stomach up and down in an obscene gesture as if he were driving an invisible knife into his guts with every punch.

'My God,' I whispered.

'What did you say?'

'Ah, nothing.'

'Hmmn,' he muttered, turned around and, breathing hard, let himself fall with a thud onto one of the chairs.

'Now . . . I mean, now that I know everything, what's going to happen to me? Why have you told me all this?'

McEnroe stared at his fingernails, Buchan fixed his gaze on his immaculately clean patent leather shoes and this time, of course, Ashkenside took even longer to answer.

'We need you because you're the only one who could carry out a special mission for us,' he said.

'What kind of mission?'

The bulletproof glasses sparkled. 'We've arranged for you to meet Andrew Baldenham. He says he'll only accept you as a contact person. Roughtrade got in touch with Baldenham. Roughtrade wants to take up contact with us through him.'

'Why?'

'No idea. Perhaps the whole thing's too much for

him. Maybe he wants to get out of the vicious circle he's in. Could be he wants to offer us something. One never knows with Roughtrade.' One of the corners of his mouth twitched.

'And when should this meeting take place?'

'We don't know yet, but probably soon.'

'Where?'

Ashkenside was listening to the voice from within and was silent as usual.

'In Damascus,' McEnroe said in a sullen voice. 'Do you know the city?'

'No,' I said.

McEnroe nodded and ran his hand over his careworn brow. 'We'll make a good job of it, Kirk,' he said without much conviction.

It was three o'clock in the morning when Alice woke me, ringing her peremptory Westminster bell.

'A direct call for you, Mr Kirk,' she said in her usual cheerful voice. 'Top priority!'

'Okay,' I said drowsily, brushed my hair back from my forehead and sat myself in front of the screen, expecting to see Andrew in his wheelchair. It was Ruth.

'Are you still alive?'

'What the hell do you mean? Of course I'm alive.'

'It's very well possible in this day and age.'

'What's possible?'

'Scenes of people long since dead can be synthesised by the computer from old films and sound recordings and you'd swear they were still living. Almost every television series today has Humphrey Bogart, Marilyn Monroe or James Dean playing leading roles, and they've all been dead for over fifty years now.'

'Believe me, I'm the real thing, Ruth, alive and kicking.'

'I've got your picture on my monitor, Pete, and I can

hear your voice. It sure sounds like your voice, but I know they can simulate that, too. I also know there are companies who, for a hell of a lot of money, act as mediators and arrange calls with the dead.'

'If it makes you feel any better, Ruth, this is not "Calls from Paradise, Inc." What you see in front of you is really and truly me. And I'm genuinely alive and halfway kicking.'

'You were always so God damn sure of what's real and what's not. How can you always be so sure?'

'It's not all that difficult if you keep your head free of trivialities.'

'Oh, Pete,' she shook her head sadly. 'You always know what's real, you also always know what's done and what's not done and just how a woman should act, what's respectable.'

'Not "respectable", Ruth. Don't be unfair. Let's say what's "proper".'

'But you decide, whatever it is.'

'Did I thank you for your birthday greetings, Ruth?'

'Ah, please, Pete, whenever we get down to serious talking, you change the subject.'

'That wasn't always the case.'

'No, but you were also different. Not so sure, so . . . self-righteous.' She turned her head to the side. She had let her hair grow and wore the same curls that she had worn when we met. They made most other women look slovenly, but I loved them on her. Now she was almost a bit too old for them. She ran the back of her hand over her nose and lowered her head. 'We were both so different,' she said softly.

'And you've called me up at three o'clock in the morning to tell me that?'

'It's not even twelve o'clock here yet. Listen, it's not my fault if they've a three hour time difference in Florida . . . '

'Where are you calling from?'

'From home, of course.'

She said this as if we'd separated a week and not a year ago.

Now I recognised the linen couch. She was sitting in her white towelling bathrobe, her feet curled up under her as if she were freezing. Beside her was the wicker table with its round glass top. A pile of my unread magazines were gathering dust. She was definitely in our home in Portland.

'They wouldn't let me visit you,' she sulked. She pressed her lips together and I noticed that the wrinkles around her mouth had deepened. The lines gave her a bitter look that I hadn't noticed before.

'Who are "they"?' I asked.

'No idea, such people never tell you their names. They tried to get rid of me, but I wouldn't play their game. Finally, they took me to their spaghetti-eating Mafia boss. The bastard was as slippery as an eel! Buchan was his name, I think. The filthy pig said he was surprised at my strange request. I told him, "I'm his wife, God damn it, and I've flown here especially to see him." Then the cheeky dwarf had the gall to ask me why my sudden interest as you'd had no news from me in the past ten months. I asked him where the hell he'd got his information from and told him it wasn't true. And the pig answers that he not only knows very well it's true, but he also knows the kind of greetings I send you. The sarcastic bastard really appreciates my charming videos. I told him to his face that he was a fag and a filthy swine to boot.'

'Buchan is Head of National Security at NASA. It's amazing that he even deigned to talk to you. Perhaps he just wanted to get to know the sender of the . . . the charming videos personally.'

I couldn't help noticing the slight interference that

flickered over the screen at the mention of the word NASA. Somewhere in the pool, a hook was at work and had activated the recording equipment. I should have known. How could I be so dumb? But now it was too late.

'He said that my request couldn't be granted for security reasons. Then he mentioned something about an operation. Are you going to be operated on?'

'You misunderstood, Ruth. I'm as fit as a fiddle. No one's going to operate on me.'

'Tell me the truth, Pete!'

'It is the truth.'

'Why wouldn't they allow me to place a direct call to you until today, then? I've tried at least ten times. "Not to be reached at the moment," they told me again and again. What's happening, Pete?'

I imagined Buchan's immovable face studying the recording.

'I don't know, Ruth. And even if I did, I couldn't tell you.'

'Is it dangerous?'

'No, it's not dangerous. I've got to help a good friend who's in hot water. It's all too complicated – hardly possible to tell you in a couple of sentences . . . '

'Take care of yourself! I really worry about you. If I can help in some way or other . . . '

'That's kind of you, Ruth.'

'Sometimes, I have the feeling that we're both dead. As if someone, at sometime or other, stole our lives without us having noticed.'

I saw that she was crying, imagined Buchan's scornful grin. He hated any form of emotion. I remained silent.

'Are you coming home when it's over?'

'We'll see.'

'Please.'

'Okay,' I replied tenderly, surprised at myself.

'Good night, Pete.'

'Good night.'

I switched the connection off with a brisk movement and could feel the protective armour inside me breaking. I suddenly realised with surprise that the armour was becoming a burden.

I stared at the screen until Alice appeared and asked, 'Do you need me anymore, Mr Kirk?'

'No thanks,' I said, padded into the kitchen and got myself a can of beer out of the fridge. It was the last one and much too cold. I rolled it back and forth in the palms of my hands before tearing it open. All that was in it were three or four gulps of a revolting, metal-tasting liquid. The rest had frozen to ice. I rolled the tin over my naked chest and went into the bathroom.

'That's love, Pete,' I said to my reflection in the mirror over the bathroom sink. 'You sour old bag. Damaged pride was not enough, now you're choked with emotion and self-pity.'

I stuck my finger into my throat and threw the stale beer up into the sink, rinsed my mouth and turned off the light.

What had she meant by "real", I asked myself as I lay in bed. But before I could gather my thoughts, I had fallen asleep.

I dreamed of the man with the slashed face that I had met on the Sultan Ahmet. He nodded to me in a friendly manner, flashing his gold teeth. His face, horribly scarred and wrinkled, was frozen into a grotesque mask. It was shaded by a soft, wide-brimmed hat and seemed distorted as if I were looking at him through a fish-eye lens. His appallingly large hands clutched the tin sugar bowl and shoved it across the counter to me – slowly – as if in slow motion. When I tipped the lid open, I was looking into Ruth's face, her mouth opened and . . .

I awoke with a scream, got up and staggered to the window. I tore it open and gasped for air. The day had dawned a murky grey. The wind had changed and was blowing in from the lagoons. The air was sultry and stifling. It smelled of carrion and polluted water. The screams of the seagulls sounded shrill and excited.

11

The Relics of an Ancient City

From now on you'll be constantly followed, McEnroe had said. One or two of my men will always keep an eye on you. They'll take turns and you won't know who they are. They'll only be in contact with you directly, if absolutely necessary.

I made the rounds of the almost fully-booked jumbo six or seven times before I discovered my two guardian angels. Both were at the back of the plane, so they could take action if anything happened up front. One of the men was a dark-haired man in his mid-thirties in a brown suit. With his black attaché case on his lap, he was obviously playing the role of the travelling businessman. Every time I went by, he pretended to be diligently studying the newspapers he had spread out over his case. The other – perhaps forty, had short-cropped ash-blond hair, tweed jacket, blue and white check shirt – also had his attaché case on his lap. He sat near the back left-hand emergency exit, his legs stretched out. Whenever I looked at him, he turned away and stared out the window, feigning interest, although there was nothing to see but a cover of grey clouds spreading over the entire North Atlantic.

McEnroe, I said to myself triumphantly, I'll be able to tell you to the man who my airplane companions are! However, both of them got off in Rome. I gave up playing detective.

Ten p.m. local time. Leonardo da Vinci Airport. Armoured cars took up their position. Soldiers in battle dress, armed with submachine guns, surrounded the plane. Security measures had obviously been stepped up. North Africa is not far. A bomb threat? Everyone has to get off the plane. A breath of early spring is in the air.

All the luggage is unloaded and must be identified piece by piece. Men in rusty red overalls, hand-sized identification papers with coloured photos hanging from their necks. Peasant faces, rigid with their official importance, all alike, patiently heave the luggage onto low carts.

Two hours later we are allowed to board the plane again. The ailing are bedded down in the front rows. Dark-skinned figures, old and frail, dressed only in their pyjamas and wrapped in blankets.

Two young men in black suits and sturdy shoes carry an old man onto the plane. His grandchildren? Breathing heavily, they lug the emaciated brown body, grabbing him awkwardly by the legs and shoulders. One of the young men lets go too soon and the old man hits his head on the arm rest. He lets out a soft cry. The young fool, adding insult to injury, steps on his hand that has fallen lifelessly to the ground. A steward arrives to take over and sends the two young men to the back of the plane. The old man looks up gratefully. His pyjama has slipped down. I see a fresh scar through the clear film of his bandage. It began underneath his heart and crossed his whole body to the right side. His eyes are turbid from pain and drugs.

'They're Syrians, not Palestinians,' the steward explains as if to calm my worries.

I shrug my shoulders

We roll to the start. The armoured cars flank us again. The barrels of the submachine guns are pointed into the darkness of the night beyond the beacons. As the jumbo gains speed, our escorts remain behind. Immediately after take-off, our plane takes a steep left curve to get out of the air lane as quickly as possible. Perhaps the pilot is afraid of gunfire from the ground.

Rome is a sea of lights although it is long past midnight. Right in the centre, spread out over the whole city, is the melancholy stone bosom of the Vatican.

The peaks of the Antilebanon loom above the thunder-clouds like bright reefs in the moonlight. Sheet lightning flashes and fills the valleys.

The plane takes a wide sweep over the desert, shaken by violent turbulences. It prepares to land. A ghostlike blue all around us – the runway lights – like being poised over a field of violets. We land at last, faltering and rumbling.

DAMASCUS INT. AIRPORT can be seen in life-sized illuminated letters at the top of the airport building. It is a two-storey functional structure with a touch of the Alhambra.

A hot dusty wind sweeps down from the Golan Heights, harbinger of an impending thunderstorm. The airships of the Arabian Commercial Line, which usually resemble proud flying palaces out of the Arabian Nights, as they are covered over completely with colourful ornaments, now tug at their anchoring like Chinese dragons gone wild. The ground crew have trouble trying to hold them down and secured them with additional lines.

'You don't need to worry about your luggage, Mr Kirk,' a short fat man said to me. 'Someone's coming to pick us up.' He was about sixty and was wearing a dark blue blazer and grey flannel pants. He carried an old-fashioned, black briefcase and a walking stick in his hand. 'Fuller is my name,' he said and grinned at me. He brushed his long white hair back at the temples and straightened his glasses. 'I was sitting behind you all the way from Washington.'

'I know,' I said. 'And you never stopped doing crossword puzzles the whole trip.'

'Memory training,' he explained. 'Please wait here.' He turned to a uniformed airport official and pulled a folder out of his briefcase.

Damascus is the ancient hub of the Orient. I was leafing through a brochure that lay on the arrival counter for foreigners. *For more than four millennia Damascus, the crossroads of the trading routes from Africa and Europe to Asia . . . outpost of Europe . . . cradle of culture and religion . . . The political focal point of the region since the turn of the century. Damascus, the oasis of peace and friendship – after Beirut lay in ruins ravaged by a forty-year civil war, Baghdad had bled to death in never-ending feuds, Jerusalem had become a bloody place of execution of irreconcilable hatred and Cairo had decayed to an overpopulated cesspool . . . The exemplary liberal social politics of our President, who has wisely administered and enlarged the legacy of the immortal Assad . . . City of conferences and international conventions, art and culture . . . A meeting place between the Orient and the Occident . . .*

I looked at the portrait of the President hanging on every wall.

'Do you know why the leaders here have such angular skulls?' Fuller asked. 'They put flat stones under the heads of their newborn. The skull vaults out to create more room for the cerebral cortex. It's not a joke either!' he assured me, when I looked at him in doubt. 'A secret recipe. Handed on generation after generation!'

An official waved us through passport control.

In the passenger hall, groups of people were camping on the floor in spite of the early morning hour. Most of them were women, half veiled, swathed in white garments. Mothers, some unbelievably young, their sleeping children bedded on their shoulders. Slender graceful hands with thick silver bracelets on their childish wrists.

An old Syrian Air jumbo scurried over the runway and finally raised its nose to the wind. The thundering of its engine sent the glassed-in front of the lounge trembling.

Our driver was a tall, gaunt fellow about thirty, bald with sparse light-blond hair, a lean haggard face and cold blue-green eyes. He was very shy and sullen, hardly opening his mouth in greeting. The American Embassy had sent him to pick us up and take us to our hotel. Fuller and I got into the back seat of the car.

A fierce wind drives dust and shreds of plastic across the road. Hundreds of the plastic scraps remain stuck in the wire netting of the fences. Trucks, with their lights off, can be seen standing at the roadside. It starts to rain. Suddenly, a shower of black smoke filled with sparks scatters over the road. An accident? A masked figure runs in front of our car. Our driver brakes and reaches for his gun in the glove compartment. A second masked figure appears, a worker, who has pulled a sack over his head. They had been burning garbage and got caught in the rain. They are seeking refuge under a pitiful shack on the other side of the road. The man looks straight into our car and falls back, terrified, when he sees the gun pointing towards him. We drive on. The rain turns into a real downpour, illuminated by lightning flashes, making it look like white rice spilling out over the country. We pass cypress trees whipped by the wind, leafless poplars and eucalyptus trees. Ugly, flat buildings appear made of mud or grey blocks of clay, some covered with rusty corrugated iron. TV antennas sway in the wind, closely packed together, like brushwood, over the rooftops.

It has not rained in the city itself. The streets are dry

and dusty and almost deserted. In the front gardens, peach and almond trees are in bloom. When we reach our hotel, the day has dawned. The sun struggles through thick grey-brown banks of clouds thronging the horizon.

The Sheraton is not the best hotel in Damascus, but it is the traditional meeting place of Americans. It is an unsightly six-storey block built in the seventies of the last century. On the sixth floor, there are windows resembling firing slits. The double loggia of the suites hang above them like pigeon lofts stuck on as an afterthought. Then, there is the ugly arched bunker-like structure over the driveway that leads up to the hotel. As they arrive, cars disappear into its tunnel. But the hotel has one advantage. It is situated on the outskirts of the city, southwest of the Omajjaden Square, between the Faez Mansur Highway to Queneitra, the railroad line to Beirut and the Choukry Kouwatly Avenue where, one hundred years ago, Mark Twain, exhausted and with a sore behind, rode in on horseback to the Syrian metropolis from Lebanon.

McEnroe was waiting for us at the reception desk. He looked hot and tired. His face was bloated, his eyes bloodshot and his breath smelled of whisky.

'We have two suites on the sixth floor,' he said. 'You'd better stay in your room, Kirk, so I can reach you when I need you. No contacts, not even via videophone. Same holds true for the hotel attendants. If you need anything, ask Fuller. He'll get it for you. His room is next to yours. If someone knocks, he'll answer. This may seem unreasonable, but our position is very difficult.'

'Still no news from Roughtrade or Andrew?' I asked.

'No, nothing yet. But, now that you're here, we're sure to hear from them. Why don't you have a few hours' rest. Do you want some breakfast?'

'I wouldn't mind,' Fuller said. 'We had dinner some-where southeast of the Azores – a good three thousand miles from here.'

'I'll have breakfast sent up to you.'

The inside of the elevator was covered in brass plate with engravings on it. The menu on the elevator wall was encased in a copy of the Omajjaden Mosque. The suite was lavishly furnished, overgrown with exuberant potted plants, a thick carpet, enormous divans and chaise longues, leather footrests and comfortable chairs and, everywhere, an abundant profusion of silk cushions. I felt as if I were in one of the tents of the caliphs of Baghdad.

Breakfast was just as opulent. Eggplants filled with minced meat and nuts steeped in olive oil, candied eggplant with honey, white creamy goat's milk covered with oil and sprinkled with wild majoram, freshly baked unleavened bread, grapes, figs and dates. The tea was spiced with peppermint, and a touch of cinnamon improved the flavour of the coffee. My prejudice against Arabian cuisine would obviously have to be completely revised.

McEnroe woke us at noon for lunch. 'We've just received a call that could lead to a contact. Get dressed. Kirk! Take a taxi and drive to . . . ' he glanced at a note he had made on a slip of paper, 'to Jabal Kassioun. That's the mountain range to the northwest of the city. There must be a kind of amusement park there for children, terrace cafés and so on. Fuller, you follow him in another car. Take Piercy with you. They wouldn't give us an exact time. "Sometime in the course of the afternoon," they said. All clear?'

'Nothing is clear to me,' I said.

He stared at me for a moment, obviously annoyed, then he growled, 'To me neither, sportsman. But we'll see. I have a real good feeling about all this. Okay?'

'If that's enough for you.'

'It's not enough, you comedian,' he shouted haughtily. 'But when I don't know all the facts, I have to rely on my feelings – otherwise, in this job, I'd be dead by now. Understand?'

I raised my hands to silence him.

'Okay,' I said. 'Okay, okay.'

The Jabal Kassioun is a barren, ochre-coloured mountain. Radar stations, satellite antennas and transmission towers are scattered at random over it. Halfway up is a sort of terrace, where numerous Damascans gather with their children when the worst of the midday heat is over.

The parking lot becomes more and more crowded as the day draws to an end. At the autoscooters, the carousels and in the games hall, especially at the electronic slot machine game Djihad, business was already booming. Young girls sauntered around in groups. They were inquisitive, haughty and self-assured.

After I had strolled up and down in vain for more than two hours, I discovered a booth that served cooled beer. I bought two cans of Henninger and was immediately surrounded by half a dozen young boys in khaki-coloured school uniforms. I couldn't understand what had caught their interest until I realised that I was in an Islamic country, where alcohol is taboo. They were probably waiting for me to fall over in a drunken stupor like the horrible examples they had heard about in school.

I sat down at a table where children had been eating ice cream. Dead ants were swimming in the raspberry-coloured sauce at the bottom of the white plastic bowls. On the concrete wall in front of me, I discovered some old friends. Round plastic reliefs of Donald Duck and Mickey Mouse, once painted in bright colours, now defaced almost beyond recognition by wind and weather. Remains of the pop culture of the last century.

I finished my beer and, to the great disappointment of the young boys, stood up without falling over and strolled over to the edge of the terrace. There was a magnificent view of the former oasis with its seven rivers – long since turned into underground sewers and covered in concrete.

The air is hazy from the dust blowing in from the desert. A strange, shapeless sun swims in the mauve-coloured sky. It looks as if it is about to fray out and dissolve. The city of over four million inhabitants seems unreal in its light. The city – a cinnamon-coloured relief with an ochre and grey background – crust-like, as if it had crystallised out of the sand of the desert after a miraculous rainfall. Graveyards spread wildly through the city like dried-out coral beds with long, slender tombstones, as if pallid relics were thrusting their way out of the dust. Far to the east, the domes and minarets of the Omajjaden Mosque are visible in the distance.

'Right there, where you're standing, Mr Kirk, the last satrap of the Byzantine Empire bade farewell to this city in the year 635. Hercules was his name. According to legend, he is said to have wept on departing.'

A rather short man, about forty years old, with a closely cropped beard and moustache was standing beside me. He had lively dark eyes and a friendly open face. He was wearing a dark suit with a waistcoat and looked like a lawyer or a teacher. He spoke English with a slightly French accent.

'Chalid, the sword of God, emerged from the desert and with his 40,000 warriors drove off 250,000 Byzantine legionnaires at Jarmuk, fifty miles southwest of here. Damascus resisted the siege for half a year, but in the end it was forced to abandon the cause. That was the beginning of the end of Constantinople.' He spread his arms out in resignation.

'How do you know my name?'

'I'm supposed to deliver greetings to you from Mr Baldenham. He's looking forward to seeing you again.'

'How is he?'

'Not very well, but he's expected to live long enough to carry out his mission.'

'Where is he?'

'In the city.'

'Then, take me to him!'

'Be patient, Mr Kirk, we're not certain yet whether your people are the only ones following us.'

'Who's "we"?'

'We have a proverb, Mr Kirk: "the thirsty one who pleads for water will be granted a drink. If he asks for the well, he'll perish." Do you understand?'

'Yes. In that case I won't even bother to ask your name.'

He nodded.

'But how can I be sure that Mr Baldenham sent you?'

'He asked me to tell you the following. I don't understand what it means, but he said you would understand immediately. "Do you remember the column of fire that evening? Do you remember the fisherman and the fish who no longer sing?" '

I smiled and thought of our last evening together in Batticaloa. I remembered the man treading through the shallow water in the twilight and the column of fire. How long ago would that evening be in Andrew's memory?

'Come tomorrow at noon to Makam al-Sitt Zainab. Perhaps we'll be able to make a little more progress. Tell your friends they should stay at home.'

'I'm afraid I'm not in a position to give orders.'

'Try anyway! I don't want to attract any attention and, more important, I don't want anyone to get hurt. Take a taxi and go there alone.'

161

'What's the place called?'

'Makam al-Sitt Zainab. The burial place of Ali's daughter. A Shi'ite place of pilgrimage near the Iranian refugee camp.'

He turned and left without saying goodbye.

McEnroe snorted when I told him the story and suggested I go alone to the meeting. He glanced questioningly at Fuller, who, with an expressionless face, was sucking on the mouthpiece of a waterpipe decorated with colourful cords that he had ordered from room service.

'Do you know how to handle a gun, Kirk?'

'No, I hate weapons of any kind.'

McEnroe sighed. Fuller sniggered, opened his briefcase and pulled out a submachine gun.

'Shall I teach him how to use it?' he said.

'Sorry, but I won't touch such an instrument.'

'Hey, cut the shenanigans, Kirk!' McEnroe growled.

'They're not shenanigans. I'm dead serious.'

'Should we let him go unarmed?' he asked, turning to Fuller.

He shrugged his shoulders and put his gun back into his case. 'There's no other alternative.'

It sounded very much as if they'd worked out some plot together. Were they both trying to dupe me?

'You'll stick to your word, won't you?' I asked doubtfully.

'Of course,' McEnroe insisted. 'I'm so glad this contact's been made. I'd be crazy to jeopardise it.'

The waterpipe bubbled. The burning tobacco smelled sweet and spicy.

'Should you really meet Mr Baldenham, bring him here as quickly as possible. We'll have him taken to the American Army Hospital Douma. He needs the help of a doctor badly. And I have a lot of questions to ask him.'

*   *   *

The Makam al-Sitt is a large, walled-in quarter. An unimaginative mosque with one minaret presides over the town. The mosque is covered with rombic green and blue patterned tiles and equipped with a set of rusty loudspeakers. Over the portal of the mosque, an ugly concrete slab has been mounted. The large white face of a station clock is displayed on it. The hands of the clock are pointing to five past twelve.

Even in the bright light of the midday sun, the place has something melancholy about it, a presentiment of death. The bleakness is intensified by the hundreds of army tents in faded camouflage colours, set up in parallel rows in the desert and surrounded by rolls of barbed wire. No tree, no bush as far as the eye can see. Container trucks with drinking water in the dusty streets. Women with colourful plastic pails, dressed in black and heavily veiled, stand in line in front of the trucks. Ugly concrete washing stands. Children playing, but they too are silent, without gaiety. Young girls with scarves and ankle-length dresses.

These are the remnants of the Ayatullah's regime. During the military coup in Iran, the people took gruesome revenge on the clergy for the senseless years of bloodshed on the Gulf, for the millions of dead, mostly children, for the unfulfilled hopes after the fall of the Shah, for the terror of the Shi'ite inquisition. More than fifty thousand mullahs are said to have found their death. They were stabbed, slain, quartered and burned to death alive. The Shi'ites would never recover from the blow. The survivors were unwelcome refugees wherever they went. Syria was the only country to grant asylum to a few of them – to the mullahs and their families who had succeeded in fleeing across the Persian Gulf.

'Allah is with the true believers,' an old man said in almost perfect English. 'That was true in the days of

Zainabs and their brothers Hussein and Hassan. They relied too much on the assistance of Allah, but he stood by and watched indifferently when Prince Hussein was killed. Shi'ites!' He spat in the dust. 'They wailed their songs of hatred against the wall every evening during the Gulf War and the women proudly bore the photos of their fallen sons or pictures of Khomeini, the old scoundrel. Now they're all dead,' he said, shrugging his shoulders, 'and Allah, once again, looked on indifferently. What remains is only sorrow and grief. But, in spite of all that, many of them have become even more religious.' He raised his cane and struck the dust with it. 'Legend has it that when the world has destroyed itself, Allah shall be worshipped in the Omajjaden Mosque. Not in Mecca, not in Jerusalem and also not here.' He struck the dust again with his cane.

'Where did you learn such perfect English?'

He was shabbily dressed in black pantaloons and a patched uniform jacket. He had skilfully wound a red and white check scarf with white tassels around his head.

He raised his head as if to take a closer look at my face through his strong glasses before answering. All he had left in his lower gums was a yellowed stump of a tooth.

'My family owned a big hotel in Beirut. Many foreign tourists visited us – before the war, of course. Now I am poor and earn a pound now and then by delivering such messages. You are requested to go over to the grey delivery truck over there.' He pointed with his cane. 'Open the back door and get in. You'll meet an old friend. You don't need to run!' he called after me. 'He's waiting for you.'

'That's why!'

'Andrew!' I called as I ripped open the door, but sitting on the right side of the truck was the man from Jabal Kassioun.

'Get in, Mr Kirk, and close the door!' he said. 'We'll

take you on a little sightseeing tour of the old part of the city. I don't trust your people. They could do something foolish and end up in the hands of the wrong people.'

'Are they following me after all?'

'I don't know, but anything's possible.'

'They gave me their word . . . '

He stopped me with a wave of his hand and knocked on the back wall of the driver's cabin. The face of a young man appeared in the cabin window and nodded. We drove off.

The Souk of Damascus, the vast marketplace of the old city to the west and south of the Omajjaden Mosque seems, at first glance, to be a complicated cave-like system – old ruins from different centuries lap over one another, ancient remains of Roman and Byzantine arches – bricks, rubble, clay, wood and concrete, all incorporated into newer buildings without any plan. The streets, repeated layers of debris accumulated in the course of the centuries, are, at times, high above their original level. Thus, the earthen floors of the older houses seem to have sunk into the ground. Staircases or steep ramps lead down to underground vaults where craftsmen have their workshops. Right above our heads, only one or two yards away, the drone of the wheels of the trucks and buses can be heard as they rush by. Swarms of small cars struggle, rattling and honking, through the narrow, almost roofed-over streets, filled with exhaust fumes and infernal noise.

From one of these streets, we turned down a steep driveway into a paved courtyard, obviously owned by blacksmiths, surrounded by eight tiny, sooty workshops, one next to the other.

'We'll have to wait here for a moment,' my attendant said, when the young man driving the truck left the courtyard. A donkey was lying in front of one of the workshops, his fore and hind legs bound to be shod.

The creature seemed completely listless. Only its ears moved convulsively from time to time, when the hot iron was pressed to its hoof and a thin stream of smoke rose into the air. Two young boys were standing nearby and watching. One had a yellow ball under his arm. The other bent over when no one was watching and spat into the nostrils of the defenceless animal. It began to roll its eyes and let out a pitiful cry. The blacksmith turned around in rage and chased them off, shouting angry insults after them. The young boys ran off laughing, throwing the ball to one another.

In the next workshop, two men were kneeling on sacks of coal in front of a bright, red-hot forge with a small anvil between them. While the one, an older man with closely-cropped grey hair, held a glowing piece of iron on the anvil with one hand and formed it with his chisel, the other, a strong fellow, his face covered in sweat, hit the anvil with the sledge hammer and forced the cutting edge onto the soft metal, splitting it in two.

I watched, fascinated. My attendant noticed my interest. 'Nothing much has changed here in the past five thousand years,' he said.

One driver hurried into the courtyard with a small three-wheel truck and turned around. My attendant raised the tarpaulin and indicated that I should get in. On the floor of the truck were a few crates of drinks that we used as seats.

Twenty minutes later, after hardly making any head-way at all in torturously slow traffic, we went through the same procedure. Another courtyard, with less noise, but with the penetrating spicy fragrance of neigh-bouring coffee roasters. On the one side, there was an old two-storied cellar with bales of cotton packed up to the ceiling. On the other side, crates and cartons were piled right up to the wooden veranda on the first floor. A young woman with a small child in her arms stared down at us with sad eyes and turned away in silence when I greeted her.

In the middle of the courtyard was a fountain, covered with the dried-up leaves of a creeper vine. The edge of the low basin was decorated with tiles, blue peacocks on a turquoise-coloured background. Most of them were broken. Had this once been the factory of Persian tradesmen?

There was a shop next to the driveway where spices were offered for sale, displayed in large square tins – cumin and caraway seeds, dark, olive-coloured peppermint, the golden yellow of saffron, the dull red of paprika and the deep, rich brown of black lemons with their bitter fragrance, black and green pepper, bunches of rosemary and thyme, ginger tubers and garlic, red and brown lentils. Crystal candy was hanging beside the door, dried out on long cords like fat strings of pearls.

I automatically approached the shop to have a closer look at what the merchant had to offer. My attendant glanced at his watch. 'We'd better go into the house. Would you like some tea?'

I nodded. We entered a sort of office which was obviously being used as a storeroom. Bales of cloth were stacked on the dark shelves in the back of the room. A large, beautiful mirror hung on the wall with Arabic letters engraved on it. An old man with broad shoulders, dressed in a white ghalabia and a wine-red tarbusch sat beside an old-fashioned till. He didn't pay any attention to us at all and sat motionless, like a puppet. I sat down on one of the chairs near the window with a view over the tiny courtyard. On the other side, no farther than six yards away, was a bakery, partly underground.

'How long is this game of hide-and-seek going to last?' I asked.

'Ayman should be back any moment now,' my attendant shrugged his shoulders. 'There's a lot of traffic at this time of day.'

A young boy in torn jeans and a faded T-shirt appeared. He was carrying a wire rack with three glasses of tea hanging in it. When he served them I noticed that the man at the till must be blind as he only reacted when his hand felt the warmth of the glass. He slurped his tea down noisily.

The tea was hot and spicy, but too sweet for my taste. I looked out the window. The baker, a young man in a thin white vest, shoved the dough for large flat loaves onto the hot stone plate of the oven, his movements as quick as lightning. The loaves rose and puffed up within seconds into cushion-like forms, only to fall back flat. The laughing face of a young woman appeared in the window of the bakehouse. She held her hand in front of her mouth when she saw me, but couldn't suppress a loud giggle. The man turned around at the noise. His dark face was covered in sweat. He nodded to me with a grin, caught hold of the young woman and grabbed one of her breasts under her dress. She shrieked and tugged at his hand. He shoved her aside and folded back a white cloth covered in flour. Under this was another layer of dough.

'Please come, Mr Kirk! He's arrived!'

The young man collected the glasses of tea. My attendant shoved a coin into his hand. He thanked him with a throaty grunt.

The old man at the till also got up. He collected phlegm in his throat and, with a cawing sound, spat it out on the floor. then he gathered up his ghalabia and, in his leather sandals, shuffled with unerring steps to the door.

This time we continued in a blue van. It stopped at a dark, narrow driveway. A steep flight of stairs led to the first floor. This time the driver also got out. He was a young man, twenty years old at the most, with black curly hair and a likeable, friendly face. He was wearing an old grey track-suit and worn-out white running shoes.

'Salam,' he said and shook hands with me.

'Shalom,' I replied in return.

'That's another word for freedom,' he said. 'Are you Jewish?'

'No, American.'

'I used to think that Jews and Americans were the same,' he explained. 'That's what we were taught at school.'

'Where do you want to take Mr Baldenham?' my attendant asked me.

'Is he here?' I pointed up the stairs.

He nodded.

'To the Sheraton.'

'Ayman will take you there,' he said and raised his hand in greeting.

'Thank you,' I said and began running up the stairs, two steps at a time. I stormed into a spacious, but gloomy, living room where layers of carpets were spread out on the floor or hung from the walls.

'Stop,' a shrill voice cried.

A plump woman in a black dress sat on a sofa. There were glass cases full of porcelain on either side of her. She was staring at a television set. A half-eaten unleavened bread lay on her lap and she picked at it with her pudgy fingers.

In a scolding voice and speaking Arabic, she asked the driver what he wanted, without letting her eyes stray from the screen. The driver shouted his answer up from the bottom of the stairs. She turned her pale, bloated face towards me, pointed with a movement of her head to a curtain of wine-red plastic pearls on the other side of the room and said, 'Okay.'

'Is that you, Peter?' Andrew shouted from the other room.

'Andrew!' I called.

'At last!' he answered.

I crossed the room in three or four strides and swept the strings of pearls aside.

12

The Blades of Fear

And there he was at last – the friend whose fate had haunted me over and over again in all my nightmares. Andrew was sitting in a wheelchair make of nickel-plated steel and plastic, his face drawn with pain. Dirty blood-soaked bandages were wrapped around the stumps of his legs. His frail hands were suntanned, resting on the padded arms of the chair. A feeling of unreality overcame me. I couldn't forget the morgue, the corpse under the sheet. It was like a surrealistic film where different shots were blended into one sequence.

'You're alive,' I said, fighting back the tears.

'Yes,' he answered and smiled. 'In one of my more transitory forms of existence.'

'Where've you come from?' I asked, after we'd carried him in his wheelchair down the stairs and got him settled in the van.

'From Iran,' he said. 'Roughtrade made this copy of me himself. It's a good copy – better than it looks at the moment. I've gone through a hell of a lot to get here.'

'Why?'

'They don't trust Roughtrade anymore. His business partners suspect that he wants to change fronts. They've become very suspicious of what he's doing. The Persian military's convinced that I'm acting as some kind of intermediary officer. They tried to prevent me from leaving so that they could force the truth out of me. But the rebels brought me to the coast and across the gulf.'

The traffic was heavy. We inched along painfully and the electro-engine whined from the constant starting and stopping.

'Have you seen Roughtrade?'

'Naturally, we've talked at length together. He's confided a lot of information to me and, of course, made suggestions.'

'But why to you of all people?'

'Because he doesn't trust anyone anymore. He's accumulated a fabulous fortune. He's probably the richest man in the world. But what good does it do him? He's always on the run from the secret services, from those who begrudge his success, from his enemies and from statesmen. They all feel he has cheated and taken advantage of them, because the copies of the top scientists he delivered did not meet up to expectations. What is worse, some of the copies even refused to work on the projects or didn't live long enough. He's convinced he can only trust me. I was his right hand man during the ten years I worked for him. As a confirmed determinist, I've always stood up for him.'

'Even today?'

'Don't misunderstand me, Pete. I'm talking about his research in the field of science. He's a genius. He was always difficult and unpredictable as a person. But when it comes to getting his ideas carried out, he's cold and calculating.'

'He's a monster. Remember how often he's had you killed.' I thought of the cruel lives and deaths of Nancy Tanner. 'He deserves the electric chair!'

'According to the biography that I've been able to piece together, he's already sold nine copies of me, not counting this one. Then there are at least three or four others who've not been able to fool their way into infopool. A dozen deaths, each one probably revolting and awful. Every time one died it was my death, too, but funnily enough it hasn't affected me all that much. Not really. On the contrary, it amuses me no end that I succeeded in outwitting death so many times – as crazy as it may sound.'

'What does he hope to achieve in negotiating with government authorities? Does he think he can return to a normal way of life, scot-free? He'll be taken to court for slave-trading or God knows what.'

Andrew shook his head, smiling. 'I don't think so, Pete. On the contrary, they'll accept him with open arms. He'll probably get to another research lab, who knows? He's continued his research and developed an automatic fault-locating program, using statistical empirical values to improve the defective recordings. This means producing copies that one could stabilise medically for months, perhaps even years. Excellent for scientific purposes, for example, space projects to the outer planets or to the stars. One could send unmanned missions into space with the appropriate receiving equipment on board and, if necessary, send the required specialist on afterwards at the speed of light. Not to mention the military possibilities that could result from all this. Pete, he'll be received like the prodigal son, believe me. He's also improved the turbulence chamber.'

He noticed my blank look and continued. 'That's the reproduction unit, the synthesiser, where matter is composed according to recorded information. Just imagine a sort of 3D molecular weaving loom. The turbulence chamber is supplied with the necessary elements and basic connections after the trial run so that all the material needed is prepared and so that no . . .'

I could hear police sirens the whole time we'd been talking. They came nearer and nearer. Suddenly, our van was hit from the left and was thrust to the right. It skidded, rolling over the side of the curb, hit some object with a crash and screeched to a halt. I tried to hold onto Andrew and his wheelchair, but was swept to the floor by the jolt. The wheelchair fell over. I struggled to my feet and hammered my fists against the wall of the driver's cabin. There was no answer. Andrew groaned in pain. I tried to force the sliding door on the right side of the van open, without success. It had been jammed in the crash. Someone was trying to open it from the outside. I pushed with all my might against it. Together, we succeeded in opening it a crack. I saw a man in a khaki-coloured uniform and a submachine gun. Behind him was a sturdy grey iron railing in front of a low concrete wall.

At that moment, the van was hit again. This time the impact was even greater. Before I fell to the floor, I realised that the soldier who'd tried to get into the van had been flung against the rail. Then I heard McEnroe's voice roaring, 'Hands up! Stay away from that truck!' I squeezed myself through the crack in the door. In front of our van was a patrol car with its sirens still squealing. It had forced our van from the street. I saw a second man in uniform with a submachine gun, McEnroe screaming at him furiously, and an ambulance car that had wedged itself between our van and the patrol car.

I looked in the front of our van and saw, to my horror, our driver hanging dead over the steering wheel. He'd been shot in the head and neck. His face looked strangely small and distorted.

'Why did you shoot him?' I screamed. 'He was only a boy. He couldn't have known anything!'

'You keep out of this!' McEnroe snarled at me. 'Get into the ambulance.'

'Why was he killed? The boy didn't do anything to anybody.'

'Shut up and leave that to me! Get in, will you!' McEnroe screamed.

I walked around the van. The man in uniform, who had been flung against the railing, wiped the blood from his nose with the back of his hand and then pointed his gun at McEnroe.

'You obviously don't know what you're doing!' McEnroe thundered at him. Fuller and Piercy, the driver from the embassy, were also there. They were holding back the two men in uniforms with their guns. 'Get him out!' McEnroe ordered the medics from the ambulance. They hurried to force the sliding door open even further and lifted Andrew out. 'That's my man!' McEnroe screamed and covered Andrew, who was unconscious, with his body. McEnroe's face was pale and shone with sweat. 'This is out of your realm of authority! Why don't you clean up the God damn mess you've made here!' He pointed to the dead man.

I climbed into the ambulance after Andrew and the two medics. I felt ill. After all, the young man would not be able to outwit death.

'Shalom,' I whispered. 'Salam.'

'What's the matter?' McEnroe asked as he followed Fuller and Piercy into the ambulance. Piercy and Fuller pointed their guns out the window and covered our retreat. We drove, red light and siren wailing, to the north.

'Nothing,' I said. 'Nothing, really.'

Early the next morning, McEnroe and Piercy drove to the American Army Hospital in Douma to talk to Andrew. Fuller and I waited in our 'headquarters' at the Sheraton.

'I'm going to town,' Fuller said. 'I've got some important business to attend to.' He grinned.

'Have the security precautions been lifted now that Andrew's here?' I asked.

'You'd better stay here, Kirk,' he insisted, 'until we know what's going on.'

I stared out the window. Two young hotel attendants were sweeping the parking lot. They thought they couldn't be seen. One of them was doing a sort of pantomime. He was holding a broom in front of him and pretending to box it on the ears, his face dead serious. The other roared with laughter until someone from the reception arrived and set them to work again.

I switched on the TV and flicked through the various programmes. TV Amman was sending a film in English, but it was an absurd oldie from the eighties of the last century. *Tootsie*, with Dustin Hoffman in the female role. I switched to another channel as fast as I could and found the Muppets. But Kermit and Miss Piggy were talking Arabic. I couldn't stand it. For a moment, I toyed with the idea of having Alice run an English or American film through infopool, but it was early in the morning in London and long after midnight in the US.

I went into the other suite in order to see if McEnroe had left any newspapers or magazines lying around, but all I found was a book bound in green plastic, lying open on his night table. It was the Koran in the original Arabic with an English and French translation. The Sheraton emblem was on the front page. Was it possible that McEnroe had been reading it?

'Which, then, of the favours of your Lord will you twain deny? They will recline on couches above carpets the linings of which will be of thick brocade; and the fruits of the two Gardens will be hanging low within easy reach . . . '

There was a knock at the door. I jumped up.

'Fuller?' I asked.

A woman's voice answered in Arabic. The only word I could understand was 'Monsieur'.

I opened the door just a crack and saw a trolley with clean towels and rolls of toilet paper. An attractive, middle-aged woman in a white apron stood beside it. She curtsied.

'Come in,' I said.

While she cleaned the bathroom, I leafed through the Koran again back to the passage about the huris of paradise. As a special reward, they await the dauntless warrior of the desert in the hereafter, *'black-eyed maidens, guarded in pavilions untouched by man or jinn . . . '* – a footnote explained: *'jinn: n. pl. (Islamic mythology) order of spirits lower than angels that can appear in human or animal form and above all lure beautiful women'* – *'as if they were rubies or pearls . . . maidens with lovely black eyes, pure as pearls guarded in their shells . . . '* – I caught myself staring at the hollows of the knees of the chamber maid while she changed the sheets on the bed. She had very muscular hairy legs. Was she really a woman? I didn't feel like finding out. I closed the book and put it down again. She wasn't watching.

I fished the coded key card out of my pocket, closed the door and glanced into my suite, where Fuller and I had slept. Fuller had not yet returned. I took the elevator down to the lobby in order to buy a couple of magazines in the International Bookshop near the entrance.

In the spacious hall to the left of the elevators, some sort of event was taking place. Groups of elegantly dressed people were standing around – well-fed ladies, their figures corsetted tightly under their long satin, brocade and taffeta evening gowns, embroidered with pearls and glitter. They wore mink stoles in spite of the midsummer heat – Hitachi mink, bred in Japanese laboratories from brainless DNS recombined marten. Lots of gold and diamonds and sultry fragrances of the Orient. Portly, important-looking, middle-aged gentlemen, just barely fitting into their dinner jackets, with dark suits and silver ties, eagerly trying to be as polite as possible and not offend the ranking order. Eye-glasses were set straight and ties adjusted. Every moment was being recorded by several video cameras under the supervision of an energetic young woman. Dozens of flower arrangements, covered in plastic foil and conserved for eternity, were set up on pedestals on the walls, row upon row like banners of the Japanese guard.

I was sure that it was a reception for some flourishing industrial company or perhaps a meeting of bank managers and their wives, when a young man in a light grey ghalabia and a red tarbush approached me with a silver tray and offered me some sweets. Lying on the tray was a card in Arabic, English and French. It stated that a well-known confectioner had just opened a branch in the Sheraton. I was now witness to this memorable occasion and was therefore being rewarded with delicacies made of sugar, honey, nuts and pistachios.

As I strolled back to the elevator, a couple was walking in front of me. They had also taken part in the festivities. I couldn't understand them, but they were obviously fighting. As they entered the elevator, the woman made an impetuous gesture and her stole slid from her shoulders and fell to the floor. I was close behind her and bent down to pick it up. At that very moment, I heard a soft clinking noise just over my head. I saw a wet spot where a few transparent splinters were clinging – a glass bullet like the boarding sheriffs of airline companies use. I automatically pressed the 'close' button. Before the doors closed – it seemed like an eternity – I was just able to make out a figure standing near the main entrance, protected by tall potted plants, his gun ready to shoot. He would've had time to shoot again, but was foiled by some people struggling to get into the elevator after me. They looked at me reproachfully as the doors closed in their faces. No one seemed to notice what was happening.

I handed the woman her stole. Without interrupting his flow of words, her husband pushed the buttons for the first and second floors. I pressed the button for the sixth floor.

The elevator stopped at the first floor. The woman got out. They obviously thought they could continue their dispute through the open door, as the man held the flat of his hand on the open button.

'Come on!' I said, but he pretended not to hear. His wife's hand, weighed down with heavy golden rings, was bent like a claw. She moved it up and down again and again as if she wanted to tear his arguments to shreds. I shoved the man aside impatiently and got out to call one of the other elevators. I pressed the button. What if that man was following me? I could be looking into the barrel of his gun when the elevator door opened. I hurried down the corridor to the right. I knew there was a tennis court and a swimming pool on the terrace in the one-storey building of the administrative section at the back of the hotel. A swinging door led to a bleak ugly corridor which linked the terrace with the stairway behind the elevators. The glass door to the terrace was locked.

This got me into a real panic. When I heard steps from below, I ran up the stairs to the second floor and when they followed, I hurried on up to the fourth floor. I peered into the hall and saw one elevator opening. A man got out and glanced around, as if looking for someone. I retreated. He was a big guy with a tweed jacket and dark grey pants. He was certainly not a native of Damascus. Was he the one who had tried to shoot me? Perhaps a professional killer? I peered again into the hall. He didn't get off. I hurried to the elevators and pressed all three buttons and rushed to the door at the staircase. I could hear steps over my head. Damn it all! Of course, he had taken a shortcut and was waiting for me on the sixth floor!

A bell rang – the doors of an elevator opened slowly. No one got off. I approached the elevator cautiously. The doors started closing again. I took a leap to reach the light barrier and recoiled in fright. A figure was lying curled up in the corner. It was Fuller! Good God!

The elevator went down. But where had it come from? From downstairs or upstairs? I was caught. The killer could be lurking on every floor. All he had to do

was put his finger on the call button and wait until the
door opened. Bang!

I rattled at all the doors along the corridor. All locked.
I knocked. No reaction. I hurried back to the stairway. A
man's voice called out from below, in a questioning
voice. In French? Someone else answered from above.
Were there two killers? One below, the other above me?
I tried to think, absolutely desperate. I had to get out of
this damn hotel. There was only one tiny possibility.
Without hesitating any longer, I pressed the call button
and flattened myself close to the wall near the elevators
and waited. One arrived. The doors opened. I looked
warily into it. It was empty.

I jumped in and flicked the 'stop' switch, released my
eraser from my wrist and prayed to God that the
impulse would hit the program storage and erase the
calls from all the other floors. I pressed the tiny piece of
equipment against the call button plate and activated it.
Then I flicked the 'stop' switch back and pressed the
button for the 'lobby'. None of the other buttons lit up,
but I'd never paid much attention to whether they'd
ever indicated calls from the individual floors. The
doors closed and the elevator started on its downward
journey. I held my breath. Third floor – the elevator
didn't stop – second – first – thank God! I breathed a
sigh of relief. I flattened myself to one side of the
elevator against the carved brass panelling. The doors
opened. I was able to examine the lobby in the elevator
mirror. As far as I could see, there was no danger. I shot
out like a flash.

All hell was loose. Fuller had been pulled out of the
elevator. He was lying on his back on the striped yellow
and brown carpet between the two elevators near one of
the knee-high black ashtrays. Someone had covered his
face and the upper part of his body with a white table
cloth and had folded his hands over his stomach. He
was surrounded by a gaping crowd. Hotel attendants

tried to hold them back, halfheartedly. The confectioner's party had taken on a macabre tone. I forced my way through the crowd to the exit. No one paid any attention to me.

Luckily some passengers were just getting out of a taxi and I got in.

'Where to?' the driver asked. I looked at him blankly. Where did I want to go?

'Drive me to town!' I said.

'To the Main Post Office?'

'Yes, to the Main Post Office.'

The Main Post Office turned out to be a four-storied grey box, set back on a terrace on the S. el Jabry Boulevard. The lower part, where the customers' windows were, was an unimaginative fretwork made of an openwork brick wall. The upper floors were obviously occupied by offices. The air conditioning units hung out of the windows like menacing cannon muzzles in front of Venetian blinds, closed halfway. Scribes sat at low wooden tables under colourful umbrellas on the terrace, typing letters for their clients on very ancient typewriters. Infopool obviously didn't have many customers in this country.

The two-storey service hall was full of people. I couldn't see an infopool anywhere. To the right, at the end of the hall, I could see a few telephone booths. People were crowding around them. A few phone books lay on a pult. I needed the number of the American Army Hospital or the American Embassy in order to call McEnroe and warn him. I closed the book helplessly. It was in Arabic.

Just by chance I looked up. On the gallery across from me a man in a dark suit put his attaché case down on the balustrade and shifted it in my direction. I took cover behind a group of men and left the hall as fast as I could, forcing my way through the crowd of people pushing to get in. I looked around in panic and caught sight of the downtown office of Syrian Air in the building opposite. I knew that they spoke English. They could help me. I ran across the terrace and beat my way through the traffic to the other side. The large glass doors were locked. A young man in a short-sleeved shirt sat at a desk. I knocked on the doorpane. He got up and came to the door and pointed to the sign in both Arabic and English, CLOSED. I gestured, trying to make it clear that I wanted him to open the door, but he answered with that peculiar movement of the head that means 'no' in the Orient. I fished a ten dollar piece out of my pocket and held it up. Filled with indignation, he made a sign of refusal and returned to his desk without deigning to look at me again.

I appealed to a passerby. 'Infopool?' I asked desperately. 'Is there an infopool office here?'

'Iffopull,' the man asked at a loss.

'Telephone, telegraph, satellite.'

'Ah – telephone, telegraph.' He pointed in the direction of the S. el Jabry Boulevard.

I started running again. At the end of the street was a large, open building. It reminded me remotely of a Venetian palace. A handsome strip of dark blue faience decorated the arched windows on the upper floor. Over the clock in the middle, a Syrian flag was hanging limply from a pole. I hurried up the stairs and through the glass doors.

It was anything but infopool. I looked around – a pair of beautiful old wooden benches, tiny wickets with iron bars, the walls painted in gold and green, a splendid carved coffered ceiling with a wooden gallery running all the way around. On one of the benches, a man was sleeping. His head was wrapped in a red and white checkered scarf. He had cast off his slippers.

Suddenly I heard a muffled thud behind me. I whisked around, terrified. A man with a peaked cap was throwing bundles of documents from the gallery. Dust filled the air. A door opened and a young man with a cart appeared. He called jokingly to the other man in the gallery and began loading the bundles onto his cart.

'Do you speak English?' I asked him.

'A little.'

'I'm looking for an infopool office.'

'Right next door,' he said. 'Out of the station, to your right – the Telegraph Office in the El Nasr Avenue.'

'What's this station called?' I asked. It looked like a toy train station. 'It's the most beautiful station I've ever seen.'

'The Hedscha Station,' the young man said, smiling. He was obviously pleased. 'Amman. A train leaves from here twice a week. Mondays and Thursdays.'

I breathed a sigh of relief when Alice smiled her sweet smile at me from the screen.

'Hello, Alice, my devoted friend,' I said. ''Twas brillig, and the slithy toves did gyre and gimble in the wabe; All mimsy were the borogoves, and the mome raths outgrabe.'

'Voice test accepted. Hello, Mr Kirk. I'm glad to see you again. How are you?'

'I've just barely escaped death.'

'That's nice, Mr Kirk,' Alice said, after a moment's hesitation. The infopool computer obviously didn't have to process such remarks every day. 'What can I do for you, Sir?'

'I need a direct line to McEnroe. You should be able to find him in the American Army Hospital in Douma.'

'One moment, please.'

I glanced around. All five cabins were occupied. Half a dozen customers were waiting for one of them to be free.

'Mr McEnroe's no longer at that address. According

183

to our records, he was called back to the hotel.'

'Then try to get him at the Sheraton Hotel!'

'Which Sheraton, Mr Kirk?'

'The Sheraton here in Damascus, of course!'

It occurred to me that the word 'here' meant absolutely nothing to Alice. To her electronic omnipresence, here was everywhere. 'Here on earth?' Yes, that was more like it, although infopool also serviced outer space.

'One moment, please.'

It was almost five minutes before the angry face of McEnroe appeared on the screen. He was not in the suite but at one of the monitors near the reception.

'What's all this shit, Kirk? God, I thought you'd given up the ghost too. Where are you, man?'

'In the Telegraph Office on the El Nasr Avenue.'

'Then get right back to the hotel!'

'Ten horses couldn't drag me back to that place.'

'Don't be childish, Kirk! I've got to know exactly how the whole thing happened.'

'Fuller's dead, eh?'

'Yeah, poor guy. Some swine shot a paralysing poison into the back of his neck. Killed from behind.'

'What should I do now?'

'Keep your eyes open. Take a taxi to the Cham Palace Hotel. That's just around the corner from where you are now. I'll be there as soon as I can get away or I'll send Piercy. Okay?'

'Okay.'

From the outside, the Cham Palace looks like a supertanker ploughing its way between the Rue El Brazil and the Boulevard Port Said to the east, through the concrete jungle of the city. Inside, it's an oasis, a princely seraglio with a central courtyard. Guests can lounge comfortably around a splashing fountain, illuminated from underneath. Long tendrils hang down from the surrounding gallery forming a wall of living vegetation that, although closely packed, lets the air circulate. Water, comfort and peace – the architect had made allowances for the desert inhabitants' concept of paradise. With an arabesque lightness, staircases and bridges made of white marble with shining brass rails wind through the courtyard up to its very heights. They seem to lead through the green of the tendrils, straight up to heaven into Jinnet, the Moslem paradise. And, in fact, delightful huris patter over the Sziraths, the bridges to paradise, in colourful pantaloons and golden, high-heeled patent leather shoes. Their elfin caramel-coloured hands, covered in jewels, sliding over the shining brass rails. Tiny golden coins clink softly from the hems of the coquettishly draped chadors, their glances fiery-eyed and emancipated. Waiters dressed in splendid red uniforms scurry up and down the staircases like tartar princes balancing silver tablets on their fingertips.

The reception hall had also tried to imitate the luxury hoped for in paradise. There were three infopool connections made of gold and ivory – ambassadors of polished brass and white plastic.

I ordered a coffee and chose a seat where I could keep my eye on the entrance. I couldn't concentrate on reading. Every time the door opened, I was terrified to death.

More than an hour later, when it was already dark outside, McEnroe came waddling in. He was exhausted and in a bad mood.

'How the hell could that have happened?' he growled. 'I left absolute instructions that you were not to leave your room.'

'Just a minute. You can't boss me around. I don't belong to your club. And, if I remember correctly, I never asked for this job.'

'That's of no importance. You've got to follow my

instructions. You ought to realise by now that such security measures are not made for fun!' He ordered a beer.

'I'd be a dead man now if I'd have stayed in my room. They'd have forced their way in somehow.'

'Or Fuller would still be alive. Those swine killed him from behind when he was out looking for you. Why did Fuller let you out of the room anyway?'

'He was gone the whole time.'

'What? He was gone?' McEnroe asked in amazement. 'So he was responsible for this shit himself!' He gulped the beer down in one full swig. 'I hope he was in the brothel again.' He burped. 'I hope so for his sake – I really mean it. He loved to go there. There isn't a city in the world he hasn't screwed in. He'd even tackle a female gorilla. His active service would've been over this fall and he could've settled down to a cushy desk job somewhere.' He pounded his head with his fist. 'Why the hell didn't I have a copy made of him for this assignment?' he asked himself accusingly.

'Perhaps because you'd such a real good feeling.'

'Is that supposed to be a joke?' he flared up.

'What kind of people were they?'

'Professional killers. International gangsters. They'll do anything for money. There were probably two of them.'

'And who paid them?'

'My God, Kirk! How should I know? But I'll find out, you can be sure of that! Anyone who has the nerve to touch my men will have his balls put out of action, I promise.'

'Where are we going?' I asked when we were in the taxi. 'To Douma, to the hospital. Or do you think I want to risk this again? Next time I won't send you into the fire, I'll send you back to the States. We'll have a recording made of you. When Mr Baldenham meets Roughtrade, a copy of you will accompany him.'

'Why does anyone have to be there at all?'

McEnroe shrugged his shoulders. 'Mr Baldenham has requested that you be there. He wants to have someone with him and he'd prefer you. I've discussed the whole plan with him and we've settled all the details. He suggested making a copy of you, for security reasons, long before this mess at the hotel cropped up.'

'Will Roughtrade really be there?'

'Yes.'

'He'll probably send a copy.'

'Baldenham said he'd definitely come personally. He wants to get out of this vicious circle he's in. And as a gift of peace – so to speak – he's bringing Baldenham's recording with him. It's supposed to be a better recording, using his latest processing methods. The doctors should be able to stabilise it medically.'

'Where's this meeting going to take place?'

'In the lobby of the Sheraton.'

'And when?'

'We don't know the exact time yet.'

'I don't have a good feeling at all this time,' I said.

'Neither do I,' McEnroe admitted. 'I've asked for reinforcements.'

The moon had just risen over the desert, bathing the mountains in an orange-coloured light. On both sides of the street there were barbed wire fences and low buildings. Here and there, a light was burning. Probably research institutes.

'Suppose this feeling we both have turns out to be wrong and everything works out all right,' I said. 'What happens to my copy?'

'You know what, Kirk? We'll send it to your old lady. She can play with it until it's bust.' His voice rang with laughter, but he stopped when he saw my face. 'Okay, forget it,' he said. 'Can't take a joke anymore, eh?'

'Sometimes, yes,' I said. 'But let's be serious – what really happens to the copies when they're no longer needed?'

'There are special hospitals. They're cared for there until they die. Their life expectancy is only a few weeks anyway.' He grinned. 'Sometimes they're given a little shove into the next world.'

'And if the copies keep getting better, with longer life spans?'

'Then we'll have a real problem on our hands.' He shrugged his shoulders. 'But one year or less is hardly worth worrying about.'

'As far as I can see there'll be legal problems. Who gets the wife? And the savings book?'

'They've already thought about all that. Copies of living persons will only be allowed in very exceptional cases. Normally, the copies will only be produced after the original has died. They've even found an appropriate name for the law: it's called the "Lazarus Act". Besides, I don't believe they'll be able to prolong life expectancy. It's been proven quite clearly that a certain error ratio has to be expected when recording as well as when copying . . . '

'I've heard all that before, but Andrew is of another opinion and Roughtrade, too, obviously. Roughtrade's supposed to have developed an error search program that could cut down the error ratio considerably.'

'Yeah, but he hasn't delivered the proof yet.'

'Perhaps he'll bring it back with him. Perhaps he'll use it to buy his way back into society?'

'If I know the gentleman responsible, he'll succeed. Wanna bet, Kirk?'

I was put into a plast-moulding tub. The substance in it was to solidify and hold the contours of my body during this 'reading' process. This is where the copy would be made, woven together in the turbulence chamber according to a flood of data from the ULT crystal storage. The recording equipment was made of chrome and plastic and looked like a computer tomograph. Laser-controlled, it could glide over the tub, vibration-free.

I didn't feel anything during the recording procedure itself, because I was under anaesthetic. They wanted to be absolutely sure no involuntary body movements occurred. I thought I could remember strange flashes of light that quivered through my brain – flurries of different coloured sparks flying here and there through my powers of perception, one after the other like tracer ammunition or exploding to form fan-shaped cascades in an afterglow of firework rockets. Probably a neurogenic storm stimulated by the scanning beams that duplicated the body layer for layer, cell for cell, to the depths of all the molecules and atoms, changing them into a digital data stream to be processed by the computer, before it became the gallium arsine crystal which cooled to almost zero Kelvin and solidified in the crystal lattice.

That night I dreamed of bright flashing laser beams like glittering knitting needles, weaving colourful, slippery hydrocarbon chains into a complicated texture, and then to flowing purple carpets, living cell formations. Vibrating, these would swell up and shrink back, sliding out of focus to form hazy labyrinths of flickering, flowing plasma, overlapping into one another, convulsing and springing back into focus. Cells, in whose plasma containers dark cores twitched, joining together and piling up, one on top of the other, like prefabricated parts of a fantastic construction site in a slow-motion film – to walls and ledges, to swelling arches and cupolas, to a breathing ocean.

I awoke with an agonising headache. I was surrounded by the most modern medical equipment. Was it an intensive care unit? Obviously, the scanning procedure had not been as simple as they'd assured me.

A young doctor came in. He winked at me in a friendly manner, but was really only interested in the instruments.

'How do you feel?'

'Lousy.' I answered truthfully.

He shook his head in sympathy. 'You've just given birth to a splendid twin.'

'Listen, joker, have you got something for my headache?'

'Sure.' He was carrying a hypodermic pistol in the halter of his belt like a sheriff carries his colt. He turned the selection disk and gave me a shot in my upper arm. Then he freed me from the sensors of the measuring instruments.

'Where are my things?'

'They'll be brought to you in a while. Please stay put. Some people react to the anaesthetic. By the way, there's a visitor for you.'

'A vicious-looking bulldog or someone in a wheel-chair with his legs amputated?'

'Neither, nor. A very pretty woman in her prime. But only ten minutes. You need to sleep off the anaesthetic.'

'Your solicitude is overwhelming!'

He winked again and opened the door. I raised my head.

'Ruth?' I asked in amazement.

She threw her trenchcoat over the foot of the bed and sat down beside me.

'What's happened, Pete? Are you ill?'

'No, only slightly indisposed – since this morning.'

'And that's why you're here in this intensive care unit? Come on, tell me the truth!'

'It is the truth, Ruth. Some kind of . . . ah . . . examination took place yesterday. And this morning I woke up here.'

'Will you tell me what's going on?' she asked. 'Tuesday they called me to tell me that I could pick you up in Damascus and take you home. I took the quickest route here and find you in this God damn hospital. What the hell's going on?'

'Did you say Tuesday? Today is Tuesday.'

'Are you trying to drive me crazy? Today is Thursday.'

I shook my head in disbelief.

'Who called you?'

'Someone from the American Embassy here. McEvans or something like that.'

'McEnroe?'

'Possibly. He said you'd be happy to see me.'

'I am happy to see you – really.'

She bent over and touched my mouth lightly with her lips. I wound a lock of her hair around my finger and pulled her head down.

When I closed my eyes, I saw flashes of light in my head, but this time it was more like lightning. I opened my eyes and saw her smiling face bent over me.

'You look tired,' she said.

'You do, too.'

'No wonder. I've been travelling for more than twenty-four hours to get here. My luggage is still at the airport. I went to the embassy and came here immediately.'

'Take a room at the Cham Palace. It's a nice hotel. I'll get there as soon as they give me back my clothes and let me leave.'

'Take care!'

I nodded.

'When am I ever going to get my clothes back?' I asked the doctor who was standing in the doorway and demonstrably looking at his watch.

'That's not my job,' he said.

Ruth took her trenchcoat and went to the door.

'See you soon!'

'See you soon!'

*   *   *

'Those aren't my clothes, nurse,' I said. 'There must be some mistake. Where's my wallet, my eraser, my watch?'

'They told me to bring you these clothes.'

'Then take them back, God damn it, and ask them where my clothes are,' I shouted, enraged at such stupidity and pigheadedness. 'They must be able to find out where they've put my clothes!'

I swung myself out of bed and wanted to get up, but my legs wouldn't cooperate. I sank back onto the edge of the bed. I was dizzy and my head throbbed madly. What had that idiot injected into my arm?

'Welcome!' a familiar voice said at the door. With thrusting arm movements, Andrew steered his wheelchair into the room and locked the door behind him. 'Do you know what they'd call us in ancient Rome? Morituri. "The doomed ones".'

'Why's that?'

'Because they're thinking of sacrificing us.'

'You mean the meeting with Roughtr . . . ' I stuttered. I could feel an icy blade touching my heart. *No! Not me! Why me?* Now I realised why I hadn't got my clothes back. They belonged to the other one! The luckier one!

Andrew watched my growing horror. 'Oh God! Didn't they tell you you're a copy?'

I shook my head and couldn't utter a sound. My head was swimming. I sank back into my pillows with a groan.

'We data replicants are born as naked as the rest of mankind. We still have to go through the shock of birth, Pete. The difference is, as an adult you're more conscious of what's happening – the consciousness of our own short existence. That's what makes it so terrible.'

He rolled his wheelchair to the sink and filled a glass

with water. He handed it to me. I sat up and drank it
down in one gulp.

'Nothing is more terrible than undisguised reality,' he
continued. 'Nothing is more unreal than reality in the
presence of approaching inevitable death.'

'You've gone through it often enough.'

'That was not really me. But I know that each time
I've felt this animal fear. It's as if I were entering
purgatory and realise there's no way back. One has to
go through with it.'

I looked down at my knees shaking in my thin cotton
pyjamas, but I couldn't stop them. Would they at least
allow Ruth to stay with me during this difficult period?
Hadn't McEnroe said as much? But she'd been told that
she could pick me up and take me with her. They could
only have meant the other one.

'And yet,' Andrew said after a while. 'And yet,
there's this feeling of satisfaction that I can always come
back and participate in this world even if it's only in this
form and . . . ' He struck his fist on the padded armrest
of his wheelchair. 'And a feeling of defiance.'

13

Roughtrade's Business

Late in the evening of the next day, an ambulance took Andrew and me to the city.

'Do you think I'll be able to see my original?' I asked.

'Definitely not. During the first few days, until the original and copy have found their own identities, they're kept apart in different environments. Sometimes strange psychic symptoms occur – unexplainable symptoms. Some believe brain interference takes place, others call it the ESP phenomenon. It sometimes occurs in identical twins. Besides, there's the shock of being confronted face to face with one's self. I can remember my first encounters in the institute.'

'Did you experiment on people there?'

'No, only on ourselves.' He lowered his eyes and was silent for a time. 'There was once a copy of me,' he didn't look up as he continued. 'It didn't live for more than an hour. A weaving mistake in the limbic system – a few highly poisonous molecules. We didn't know much at the time. I'll never forget his screams and the way he looked at me. I screamed with him and was numb for days on end. I really had the feeling I'd died with him and was just being kept alive artificially. It wasn't normal pity, it was a higher form of compassion, a literal form. There was a puzzling parallelism that evolved via immediate contact of the two brains – the original and his copy.' He shrugged his shoulders.

'Research on this phenomenon has not progressed at all.'

McEnroe was waiting for us at the entrance to the Sheraton. He greeted us as 'his parade of monsters', tactful as always. We went over to the elevator. I turned around instinctively and looked at the tall potted plants near the entrance, before I got into the elevator and rode up to the sixth floor.

We received our last instructions on Roughtrade: 'He's announced that he'll be arriving at six o'clock in the morning. At that time there are no guests in the lobby. As a signal that everything's in order, you, Mr Kirk, are to push Mr Baldenham's wheelchair out into the driveway of the hotel to meet his car. At that point Mr Roughtrade will get out and you, Mr Baldenham, will give me a sign that the man is really Roughtrade. Mr Roughtrade will take the recording of Mr Baldenham out of the trunk of the car – a large aluminium container with thirty-two storage crystals in it. He'll hand it over to you, Mr Kirk. You'll then follow Roughtrade to the entrance and into the lobby where I'll be waiting with my men, while Mr Baldenham . . . '

' . . . stops the getaway with his wheelchair and body just in case anything should happen in the driveway,' Andrew said. 'Perfectly logical.'

McEnroe gave him a sour look. 'Is everything clear?' he asked.

'Absolutely,' I said.

'Then we'd better get to bed. I've left instructions for the reception to wake us at five in the morning.'

'Hello, Rachel!' Andrew said to a young woman on the infopool screen. 'When you and my true lover meet and he plays tunes between your feet, speak no evil of the soul, nor think that body is the whole.'

'Voice test accepted, Mr Baldenham,' the dark-haired

young woman responsible for Andrew answered. 'What can I do for you?'

Andrew flicked a cassette out of his dictating machine and pressed it into the slot of the infopool monitor. 'To myself. Sound transmission. Start.' He touched the sensor. 'Even if our lives are short and fleeting,' he said, turning to me, 'I want to keep track of it, just in case something really does happen tomorrow.'

'Do you think anything will happen?'

He shrugged his shoulders, 'Yes.'

'Then Roughtrade is also in great danger.'

'He's prepared for that. He has many enemies. After all, he knows a hell of a lot about politicians in the Third World. They now live in perpetual fear of being exposed to their disadvantage. That's the only reason our top officials are so interested in him. Such information leads automatically to blackmail and political pressure.'

'But what if the real Roughtrade decides to come? What a risk!'

'Then it's a risk he's calculated. You shouldn't under-estimate Roughtrade – he's as cold-blooded as he's brilliant.'

The monitor spat out the cassette. Andrew held it up between two fingers. 'Taking a look at my biography, Pete, I realise I'm a strange time traveller. Like a hunted animal on the banks of a river called time. An impression here, half of one there, an unturned stone, a torn-off leaf. On it goes! Sometimes here, sometimes there! Long past and over!'

'Do you need me anymore, Mr Baldenham?' Rachel asked.

'No, that's all for today.'

For a moment I toyed with the idea of getting Alice on the screen and, in spite of it being expressly forbidden, asking for a direct line to my alter ego. But the very thought of facing him made me decide against it.

'Do you still need the cassette?' I asked.

'No.'

I stuck it into the dictating machine and switched it on. 'Then we should not let this, possibly our last evening together, fall into oblivion.'

'For whom?'

'For my alter ego.'

'Whatever we talk about, Pete, McEnroe will have it censored and won't let it through.'

'And your message?'

'I got his permission, with Buchan's approval.'

'I'll hide the cassette then.'

'How will your original know you made a recording and hid it?'

'I'll see that he gets the message.'

'From whom?'

'From McEnroe personally.'

'You know very well he expressly forbade you to have any contact. He'll never do it.'

'Wanna bet?'

I looked around the suite, but my luggage was no longer there. My glance fell on Fuller's briefcase. I opened it and rummaged around in his belongings. I found his dictating machine between crossword puzzles and porno magazines. I made sure it was still in working order, put it down beside Andrew and switched it on.

'Aha,' Andrew said and raised his finger, 'I understand redundancy.'

I nodded. 'Exactly.'

'Pass me an orange, please,' Andrew requested.

I got an orange out of the bowl of fruit on the table and handed it to him. I took a couple of grapes. The almost plum-like, dark-blue grapes tasted very strange, somehow soapy and bitter.

'There's something wrong with my sense of taste.' I spat them out in the ashtray in disgust.

'Possibly a flaw in your brain. It's very complicated,

you know. The probability of discrepancies in reproduction are correspondingly large. The consequences are more serious – not only in the cerebral cortex and the interbrain, but especially in the brain stem.'

'They'll never be able to completely avoid such errors.'

'That's not the point. Strictly speaking, all living organisms are liable to reading errors. The error ratio has to be low enough so that only an insignificant part of the population is incapable of living. The same theory is valid for data clones.'

'I thought it'd been proved that . . .'

'There's a mere supposition by a couple of randomists in chaos research, Horace Simonson and Aron Rosenblueth, both students of Alan Garfinkel of UCLA. They claim that analogous to the Heisenberg uncertainty principle in the subnuclear sphere, there's something similar in the molecular sphere – for the conversion of matter into information and back. I don't believe in either. I'm a confirmed determinist like Roughtrade. I don't believe in the fundamental limitations of perception. We'll never know everything, because facts are infinite. Just because statements of facts are facts doesn't mean that, in principle, whole areas aren't closed to perception or discovery.

'You know, Pete, the brain is a fantastic organ that, in the course of billions of years, has been developed into a perfect instrument – not to discover the world, but to survive in it. This means that whole groups of facts will be filtered if they are not absolutely biologically relevant – so that our organisms can devote more of their time to the biologically relevant ones. What really is behind our outer selves is a puzzling, incredible and damn indifferent world.

'Is it any wonder if we, with our limited powers of perception, come up against hurdles that seem insurmountable? I think it is too early to talk about fundamental limits. There are only limited recordings, incompetent measuring methods and inadequate instruments.

'I believe that this universe is ruled by the laws of cause and effect. It wouldn't exist otherwise. Roughtrade is right when he describes his opponents as mystics. I believe in the indivisibility and strength of determinism.'

'And in the resurrection of the flesh,' I added.

'And in the resurrection of the flesh. Just look at the disputes when it comes to budget deficits or government hearings! The arguments of the randomists are only considered more important because we determinists haven't progressed very far with our research. Everything was going so well, but we miscalculated the difficulties in transforming inorganic into organic matter. And without this step, the MIDAS technique's worthless. What's the good of reproducing complicated mechanical or electrical products if the copies cost ten times as much as the original? The procedure would be really interesting in the reproduction of organic substances – food out of the data storage.'

'Multimanna?'

'Multimanna. But that's where the difficulties all started. Reading errors occurred again and again. They produced poisonous substances. It was mad! We had put all our hopes in Multimanna. We wanted to eliminate hunger in the world.'

'Magic Table.'

'Do you know the fairytale?'

'I do now. "Gold Donkey" is also clear to me now – it's not worth the cost. But what is meant by "Club in the Sack"?'

'It's of great importance to the military. Recordings of a few trained specialists could be reproduced and sent to the front as needed. Research has continued in this field -- secret research. The quality of the copies is good

enough for soldiers. They only need to live long enough
to do their duty. No need for them to return from their
assignment.'

'What if they don't have the necessary motivation?'

'Motivation can be induced chemically. You only
need to stimulate the right part of the interbrain – set
into motion a fighting soldier filled with such hate he
won't deviate from his course. And if he gets bullet-
holed, you fire the next copy to your target. And if he
doesn't succeed, the next one or the one after next. An
ideal toy for generals, admirals and such strategists.' He
laughed sarcastically.

We were both silent for a long time.

'Let's get some sleep,' Andrew said.

I switched off both machines. I put one back into
Fuller's briefcase and took the cassette out of the other
and handed it back to Andrew. I looked around the
room – cupboard, night table, bed, desk, lamp, air
conditioning, wastepaper basket, divan, chaise longue,
armchair, under the carpet, in the bathroom? All too
unimaginative. I didn't want to make it easy for them. I
examined one of the potted plants. It was planted in a
container similar to a barrel and the staves of the barrel
formed a hollow space under the plant. I shoved the
cassette into the space and straightened the plant.

I helped Andrew to the bathroom, then heaved him
out of his wheelchair onto his bed. He was light as a
feather.

Later, as I lay in bed, I trembled with fear and my
heart started beating frantically. I held my breath to
suppress a moan. Finally, the seizure subsided.

'Are we real?'

'A highly philosophical question,' Andrew answered.
'I'll have to sleep on it.'

'That reminds me – did you know there is a legend
that says that when the world has destroyed itself, Allah
shall be worshipped in the Omajjaden Mosque.'

'If the Omajjaden Mosque still exists and a human soul to worship in it.'

We were silent for a long time.

'Have we got a soul, Andrew?' I asked.

He didn't answer and I thought he'd fallen asleep, but then I heard him turn over in bed.

'An interesting question,' he said. 'Is the soul indivisible?' He laughed softly, but it sounded more like sobbing. 'Maybe that's our problem, Pete. We have no soul.'

I lay awake for a long time and struggled to understand my destiny. Why me? Why not him? What was he doing at the moment? Was he with Ruth in the Cham Palace Hotel? Was he sleeping with her? Now at this very moment? Did he waste a moment's thought on me, his ghoul, his double? I remembered what Andrew had said about interference symptoms between the copy and the original. In the almost hundred hours since the recording procedure, we had 'drifted apart'. He had long since become 'the other', had experienced, heard and seen different things.

Hello, you out there! Can you hear me? It's me, your alter ego. Every second I plunge further and further away from you. Can you hear me? Can you hear me?

I strained my ears into the blackness of the universe beyond my skin. I received no answer.

I awoke to a strange howling and moaning noise. I couldn't figure out what it was. It was daybreak. I got up and opened the window. It was the muezzins' call to morning prayer. The name of God blared, droned and rattled from hundreds of hopelessly overmodulated loudspeakers. The sound was more like the howling of a host of devils trying to capture one poor soul.

Someone knocked at the door. I heard McEnroe's voice. Breakfast was rolled in. It was as sumptuous as the morning of my arrival in Damascus, but I couldn't eat a thing. I drank a cup of black coffee. Then we took the elevator down.

When we got out of the elevator, I was appalled at the feeling of nervousness that took hold of me for no reason at all. I wiped my forehead and mouth and realised that my hand was bathed in sweat. It was as if my fear would take on some kind of gruesome form and appear before me. My knees threatened to give way. But before the fear could take hold, I forced myself to fix my eyes on the hotel entrance and pushed the wheel-chair in that direction without glancing back. Half a dozen foreigners were loitering in the lobby to the left and right of the entrance. All had well-trained athletic bodies, all pretended not to be interested and yet all reacted with catlike vigilance to any movement that took place near the glass doors at the entrance. They all carried raincoats over their right arms as if the rainy season were approaching in spite of the cloudless sky. Were they copies? McEnroe glanced nervously at the computer on his wrist. He spoke into it from time to time in a low voice, giving directions to his men. He probably had some of them outside the building, too, and possibly on the roof, so they could monitor any-thing happening in the surrounding area.

I stopped and felt that I had overcome my fear and had myself under control again.

They had chosen the Sheraton because of its flat, bunker-like projecting structure over the entrance to the hotel. It offered a certain degree of safety from an outside attack. The projecting structure was built like a highway tunnel about eight to ten yards wide and broken on both sides with gallery-like archways. Foot-paths about one and a half yards wide covered with white tiles and flanked with flowerbeds containing agaves, evergreen climbers and dwarf palm trees, led through these archways to a spacious parking lot.

Behind the parking lot the ground became steep, over-grown with dense shrubbery and occasional eucalyptus trees, surrounded by a fence made of iron bars. On the other side of the Faez Mansur Street, there were several skyscrapers that had been built in the eighties and nineties and the railway line to Beirut went over the high embankment southwest of the wall.

We waited. I noticed that Andrew's intestinal haemorrhaging had started again. He had been suffer-ing from it for weeks now. A thin trickle of blood fell over the edge of his seat and ran down the chromium-plated steel of the wheelchair. 'A flaw in the weaving process,' Andrew had explained disparagingly.

Suddenly, there was a commotion. Two large, dusty Mercedes Benz stopped in the driveway. Two wiry young men in long white garments and black checkered scarves jumped out and looked around. Obviously not only chauffeurs, but also body guards. A tall, broad-shouldered Arab in a wide black coat with an aghal around his white scarf got out, followed by an older and a younger woman and children – two boys and three girls ranging in age from five to fifteen. They looked at us. Sleep was still in their dark eyes.

In a gruff voice, McEnroe tried to order the broad-shouldered Arab to have the cars driven away from the entrance. A young man from the reception translated in a whining voice, wringing his hands in supplication, but it didn't seem to impress the Arab at all. He turned away. McEnroe hurried after him. He was stopped by both bodyguards. They stood in front of him with their hands on the silver handles of the curved daggers they carried in their sashes around their waist. Suddenly, they were looking into the barrels of several submachine guns that appeared from under the trenchcoats.

The man in the black coat raised both his hands in defence, and asked in a low voice what was happening. The man at the reception answered in a submissive manner. McEnroe chased his men off. The submachine guns disappeared and the two bodyguards proceeded to unload the luggage from the cars – baskets and leather trunks, almost as large as wardrobes. McEnroe's wrist computer started blinking. Almost simultaneously, a third car appeared to the left of the driveway entrance. The driver stopped when he saw the two cars parked in front of the entrance and drove on to the parking lot on the other side of the projecting structure.

'That's him!' Andrew called.

McEnroe looked around desperately. 'Get going!' he shouted angrily. He knew that he'd made a terrible mistake in not having the driveway closed to all other cars, but he hadn't expected cars at such an early hour. I pushed the wheelchair to the entrance and continued on between the two Mercedes Benz to the footpath that led to the parking lot. A tall, slender, grey-haired man in an elegant, dark blue suit got out of the car, walked to the back and opened the trunk. He lifted a large aluminium container out of the trunk and closed it.

'Cecil!' Andrew called.

He seemed genuinely pleased to see the bastard, I thought. The monster – putting him through hell so often just to earn a fortune for himself.

The man raised his hand in greeting and, suddenly, several things began happening all at once. Roughtrade held the aluminium container up and slung it from him with such a violent movement that the whole weight of his spine thrust him forward and his legs buckled under him. Blood gushed forth from several holes in his chest. The suitcase bounced on the ground two or three times before white smoke welled up from it. I heard shots and out of the corner of my eye could see muzzle flash flare up at two points on the wall. McEnroe roared, 'Take cover!' But before I could react, Andrew's head exploded in front of my very eyes and splashed all over my chest and chin. I felt a blow and, without any warning, found myself lying on my back on a small piece of lawn between flowers and bushes. The wheelchair was four or five yards away from me. Andrew hung to one side over it. The upper part of his head had been blown off. I could hear rifle shots behind me and bursts of fire from submachine guns. I was too weak to struggle to my feet. I looked at my arms in amazement. They were covered in blood. Then someone grabbed me between my shoulder blades and pulled me up. I was suddenly on my feet again. I ran through bushes and flowers – no, I floated. My arms and legs had become strangely numb while a fire spread wildly in my breast, consuming the air in my lungs and filling my eyes with black smoke so that I couldn't see . . .

I stood by and observed how he was hurled into the flowerbeds and then disappeared behind the gallery out of my field of vision. He emerged again and staggered through the bushes until he fell and remained lying, his face buried in a bed of orange-coloured flowers. I reeled against a pillar in the lobby of the hotel and would have fainted, but the pillar supported me. I looked at my arms and chest – for a moment I was certain they were stained in blood.

'Are you wounded?' one of McEnroe's men asked angrily.

'No,' I gasped, but felt pain in my chest as if I'd been hit, and not the other one that they'd sent out in my place.

A long, harrowing scream came from the railway embankment to the southwest of the wall. Then, the shooting noises died away. All that could be heard was the crying of the terrified children, cringing with their mother behind their luggage.

I could hear McEnroe calling out, 'The coast is clear! There must have been at least two of them!' He and his men and the two bodyguards had sought cover behind the cars parked in the entrance.

He emerged, his face flushed with anger, an aluminium container full of bullet holes in his hand. A thick white crust had formed around the bullet holes.

'What a damn mess!' he growled. 'Did these camel drivers have to get in our way?' Furious, he threw the container down on the floor beside an armchair. 'You stay here, Kirk, until they've cleaned up this mess. You'd better go upstairs, the way you look!'

'I didn't sleep all that well last night,' I said.

'Don't put me on. I warned you. It was you who insisted on being here. Some strange things have happened to men whose copies died, I tell ya!'

It was worse than I could ever have imagined! I was conscious of him before I saw him, felt his nervousness and fear. Then he got out of the elevator, pushing Andrew in his wheelchair in front of him. I thanked God that he wasn't looking in my direction. I could never have looked him straight in the eye. I was conscious of how my nervousness was transmitted to him. He probably wasn't aware of it because he had a goal to reach. I saw how his movements became more erratic. How well I knew those gestures, my gestures – my hand brushing my forehead and wiping my mouth, that dry swallowing, the back movement of my head. I caught myself imitating them like his reflection in the mirror. I was conscious of how his growing nervousness flooded back to me, how a neurological feedback was set into motion and threatened to overpower me. I didn't tell McEnroe about the horrible dream I'd had the night before.

I was wandering through the Souk, looking into the storerooms and warehouses brimming over with goods, into the offices, into the tea and workshops, into the underground blacksmith's and baker's. There wasn't a soul anywhere. It was cold and everything was covered with dust and ashes. Insects were swarming in the gloomy cellars of the tradesmen, salvaging the useless goods for the future of their world. I called into the stillness again and again, but no one answered. Then I came to the Omajjaden Mosque. There they were, all lying prostrated on the ground, filling the large carpet-covered area around the tomb of John the Baptist, packing the courtyard between the arcades and lying one beside the other – the blacksmiths, the spice dealers, the porters alongside the smartly dressed gentlemen from the confectioner's party, all lay there pointing to the south, body on body. They were all dead, their putrifying foreheads touching the ground.

Then I heard my alter ego, shouting in my voice, 'Hello, you out there, can you hear me? I'm you, your other self. Every second, I plunge further and further away from you. Can you hear me? Can you hear me?' And it was as if he were speaking out of the depths of the earth and foundered with every word deeper and deeper into the earth. I awoke and was terrified.

I took the elevator up to the sixth floor. The door of the suite, where my copy and Andrew had slept the night before, was only leaned to. Just as I was about to open it, a young man with a video camera came out.

'You can't come in here!' he said. I seized him by his lapels and shouted, 'You clown! I live here. What are you doing in my room?'

He stared at me in a daze and raised his hands in appeasement. 'Okay, okay, Mr Kirk!' But he continued to block my way. 'Search for clues concluded,' he spoke into his wrist computer. 'Mr Kirk is here. Can he . . . ? Okay.' He indicated that I could enter the room.

'Bureaucratic asshole!' I said and slammed the door in his face. He pressed his camera protectively against his chest.

What kind of clues had they found? I looked around

the room. Had my alter ego left a message for me? Where could he've hidden it? Cupboard, night table, bed, desk, lamp, air conditioning unit, wastepaper basket, divan, chaise longue, chair, under the carpets? In the bathroom? He wouldn't have had so little imagination. I examined one of the potted plants.

'You're very hot, Kirk!' McEnroe stood behind me and was holding the cassette of the dictaphone in his hand. 'Where would you've hidden it?'

I shrugged my shoulders. The plant was in a barrel-like container, the staves of which formed a small space between the plant and the floor. 'Perhaps under it.'

'You electronic twins are better tuned to one another than quartz clocks,' he said enthusiastically. 'Very nice. But I'd have expected a little more of a telemetry engineer.'

I raised my shoulders. My glance fell on Fuller's briefcase, which was leaning beside a chair. Suddenly, the word 'redundancy' occurred to me. I let my glance wander on carelessly and opened the door.

'I've got to listen to his last greetings, Kirk. Sorry, but I forbade any contact whatsoever.'

We went into the other room of the suite. There were three aluminium containers in the middle of the room, all exactly alike, just like the one that had been shot full of bullet holes that McEnroe had deposited beside the chair in the lobby.

'What are those?' I asked.

'ULT-containers used for transporting storage crystals of recordings. They were delivered this morning. I don't know what's in them. If there was an important recording in the other one, I'm in trouble.'

When McEnroe went downstairs, I opened a beer, then wandered back to the other room, sat down in a chair, put Fuller's briefcase on my lap and opened it. Between crossword puzzles and porno magazines, I found his dictaphone. I wound it back and played it.

'Aha!' Andrew said. 'I understand – redundancy.'

'Exactly,' my copy said.

I pulled the cassette out and put it in my pocket. I let the dictaphone fall back into the briefcase. I closed it and put it down near the chair. Then I drank my beer slowly before going down to the lobby again.

They were just on the point of carrying the dead bodies off. In the parking lot, five flat black coffins were lined up in a row. On one of them, someone had written 'Kirk' in chalk and below the name was a 'C', probably for copy. There were question marks on the other two coffins. Then they were all hoisted onto an American army ambulance. Another car had gone ahead with two wounded. A few local and military police cars were still waiting at the parking lot. Armed men in khaki-coloured uniforms had taken up position at the exit and entrance to the driveway.

McEnroe's men were nervous and depressed. A third assailant had obviously got away. A third weapon had been found to the southwest of the wall. The man had probably fled with an accomplice over the Faez Mansur in the direction of Quneitra.

Two of McEnroe's men had suffered bullet wounds. One was in critical condition and he wasn't a copy.

Two hotel assistants with brooms and hoses were busy trying to get rid of the remains of the battle on the tiles of the path that led to the driveway. Both were sniggering about something, but became silent when they saw me coming.

'Do you want a taxi, Sir?' one of them asked.

I stared at the black-brown stains smeared over the tiles and shook my head.

Andrew's wheelchair had been set aside carelessly in the driveway. No one had taken the trouble to remove it. McEnroe was standing with three of his men in the lobby to the right of the entrance. They were still carrying trenchcoats over their arms. I joined them.

'What kind of recording was that?' I asked and pointed to the bullet-holed aluminium container.

'How should I know?' McEnroe answered and wiped the sweat from his face with a handkerchief. 'I hope they're not the research papers he promised to bring with him. That would be a real fiasco! If the crystals are heated even a few degrees, the stored information's automatically deleted. Whatever was in that container is definitely ruined.'

'Wasn't he going to bring Andrew's recording with him?'

'How do you know that?' he asked distrustfully.

I thought about it for a moment. But I couldn't remember. 'Didn't you tell me?'

'I never told you anything like that.' He examined me apprehensively.

'I really don't know,' I said shrugging my shoulders. 'I just thought you'd told me.'

He nodded. 'Very interesting. Either you're cleverer than I thought or you've just given yourself away. Or it's one of those phenomena that I've often observed in twins like you.'

'And what's in the containers upstairs?'

'If what he said's true, they're recordings of Rough-trade and Baldenham.'

'You mean the real life-size Roughtrade died out there?'

'The doctor says so, but we're waiting for the final results of the autopsy.'

I couldn't help nodding in satisfaction.

'And in the third?'

'I pray to God,' he said and actually laid his fleshy right hand on his sweat-drenched shirt, 'that they're the research documents he told us about.'

Suddenly, I couldn't believe my eyes. Ruth was standing at the entrance, obviously searching for me. When she saw me, she hurried over. McEnroe, whose glance had followed mine, raised his hand and bellowed, 'Don't shoot!'

Ruth stopped in her tracks when she realised that the dark muzzles of the submachine guns were directed at her.

'Come here, Mrs Kirk!' McEnroe said. 'Nothing'll happen to you.'

'What's all this about?' she asked.

'An assassination took place here this morning,' he said. 'My men are still a bit nervous. Please forgive them.'

'What are you doing here, Ruth?' I asked in amazement.

She frowned at me, evidently angry. 'I rented a room in the Cham Palace Hotel like you told me to. I waited the whole God damn day for you or at least a call from you. At the army hospital, they said you were out and couldn't be reached. But infopool finally informed me that you were at the Sheraton. I phoned here again and again. Each time some asshole or other answered and said you were not in at the moment. I didn't know what to believe so I took a taxi here.'

Her eyes lit up, ready for a fight. I knew that look.

'It's so nice to have you here, Mrs Kirk,' McEnroe said, but he noticed that his patronising manner did not impress her. 'May I have them bring you a drink?'

'No thanks, Mr McEnroe, I don't want a drink.' She sat down and lit up a cigarette, intentionally ignoring the light McEnroe offered. 'All I want to know is what's going on here.'

I began to realise what'd happened.

'Ruth, I . . . '

'Excuse me, Pete, but I'd like an answer from Mr McEnroe. He's the one who invited me to Damascus.'

'Mrs Kirk,' McEnroe said. 'Certain things are so important they've got to be kept secret. But I can assure you it's all done in the name of our government and for the well-being of the American nation.'

Fearing a somewhat less patriotic remark from Ruth, I said quickly, 'Will you be needing me anymore?'

'As far as I'm concerned, you can fly back to the States.'

'Please excuse me for a moment, Ruth. I'll just get my luggage.'

'Take this broad with you, will you?' he said in a low voice as he headed with me in the direction of the elevator.

'You're talking about my wife.'

'Ahaaa,' he drawled and grinned. He opened his mouth and let the tip of his tongue hang out over his lower lip. It was horribly obscene and not at all amusing. We got into the elevator.

'Why did you have her come to Damascus at all?' I asked. I had trouble controlling my anger.

He pretended to be astonished. 'As a piece of candy for you, of course. For your unselfish dedication. I let your double have a pass at her.' He cackled with laughter. 'I was sure you wouldn't mind – judging from how broad-minded you've been in the past.'

I was furious. I tried to grab him by the shoulders and push him against the wall, but he freed himself without any effort at all. 'Don't be funny,' he said. 'Drive to the Cham Palace with her and I'll book two seats to Portland and have them delivered to you.'

'You're kindness in person, McEnroe,' I said.

He shrugged his shoulders. 'Have a few nice hours together. Let your anchor fall into home port tonight.'

' . . . and a swine to boot.'

He patted me on my shoulder in his usual patronising manner. 'That's the way I like you, boy.'

Both hotel attendants had finished their work.

Andrew's wheelchair had disappeared. Ruth's high heels clappered loudly on the pavement.

I was suddenly in a great hurry to get away from the place. I didn't look back. I put my arms around her shoulders. The wind from the barren mountains in the west was almost as hot as it was at midday. Ruth's curls were blown into her face. She looked up at me, brushed them away from her cheeks and smiled.

'When I saw you the day before yesterday,' she said, 'you seemed so unreal. It was as if I were touching someone else. Today you're real.'

Her hand found its way through my open shirt. It was cool and tender.

When we reached the tiny mosque at the northwest exit of the hotel that led to the Choukry Kouwatly, a huge white Mercedes Benz caught up with us, driving out of the Sheraton parking lot. It drove slowly alongside us. The tinted pane of the rear window rolled down. I was overcome with terror. The car stopped. I was looking into the face that had haunted me day and night since our flight on the Sultan Ahmet. The scars wrinkled into a mad smile, gold sparkled.

'I'm glad to see you're so well, Mr Kirk,' he said. 'Give Mr Baldenham my greetings should you see him again.'

'May I ask who's sending the greetings?'

'Names are sound and fury. He also only knows me as the one on the Sultan Ahmet, although we've met occasionally in his other lives.'

He nodded to Ruth and raised his hand in greeting. The tinted window rolled up automatically and the car turned south on the Choukry Kouwatly.

'Who was that for God's sake?' she shuddered.

I shrugged. 'Who knows? Perhaps a real slave trader.'

'Come off it – there aren't any nowadays.'

'I wouldn't be too sure of that.'

*   *   *

The peace of the seraglio in the Cham Palace helped us forget the hassle we'd had. I awoke in the middle of the night. Ruth's arm lay across my chest. I strained my ears into the darkness, but all I could hear was the soft whispering of the air conditioning unit. The cries of the other, who had died, were silent forever.

Two weeks after we were home in Portland, McEnroe called to tell me that he couldn't give me the cassette he'd taken away from me, because it contained top secret military information.

'You mean "Club in the Sack"?'

He looked at me in resignation. 'You were taking me for a ride, eh?'

'A basic concept of the information theory. It's called – "redundancy". I won't tell you how it works.'

He nodded. 'We won't be seeing one another anymore.'

'Oh, how sad,' I said, but he didn't catch the irony.

'I've been fired,' he explained morosely. 'I've been shoved off to a desk job.'

'Was the third container empty?'

'No, but the bullet-holed container had all the research documents in it that Washington was so keen on having.'

'A desk job also has its advantages,' I reassured him. 'Now you can concentrate all your efforts on the comparative research of data replicants.'

'As if much could be done in that field.'

'Why? You have Roughtrade.'

'If only you knew!'

A short time later, I received a call from Andrew. He'd been operated on several times. He seemed very weak and exhausted, but they'd succeeded at least in stabilising the copy to some extent. He was confident and cheerful. I promised to visit him as soon as possible.

When NASA summoned me to appear in Houston at

the beginning of May, I took the roundabout way via Los Angeles and visited him in Pasadena.

It was one of those hospitals that McEnroe had told me about. Electronic clones were wasting away from mysterious physical and intellectual afflictions. They had the undivided attention of science. The hospital was set off in a spacious park surrounded by old trees. It had been modelled after a seventeenth-century French castle and built by a Hollywood millionaire in the sixties of the last century. Low sterile white medical laboratories cowered between high bushes in the shade of old plane and pine trees.

When I drove into the parking lot near the entrance, a stout, white-haired man stepped out of the gatekeeper's hut. He hobbled towards me, supporting himself on a sturdy cane. Its stud was a silver skull.

'Drive here into the shade, mister,' he called, and pointed the skull in the direction of a tall pine tree that loomed behind the hut. When the man turned his head, I noticed that he'd been badly burned on his right temple. His ear was a small, white, shrivelled piece of gristle. His eyebrows and hairline had been burned away, his skin shone smooth and rosy, stretching tight over the temples. I noticed that his right leg was extremely short and turned outwards, but he moved skilfully with powerful flowing movements.

I parked the car, got out and locked it. I turned around and stopped in amazement.

'Mr McEnroe?' I asked, uncertain.

He looked at me sternly. His right eye, injured by the burns on his temple, had sunk lower into his face than the left one.

'Do I know you?' he asked.

I shrugged. 'I . . . I'm not sure.'

All of a sudden, he grinned. 'You probably know my original,' he said. 'Greet the old bastard for me and tell him I'm still living – against all expectations.' He tucked his cane under his arm, took a crumpled cigar stub from the windowledge of the hut and lit it with an army lighter. 'You know,' he said, puffing, 'that guy hasn't had the guts to come and visit me. Not even sent a bottle of whisky or a couple of cigars. And I went through hell for him.' He puffed an immense cloud of smoke. 'And it was damn hot, I tell you. Napalm.' He pointed to his temple and seemed fascinated by the embers on the stub of his cigar. 'Give me a hundred dollars, mister?'

'Bit much for just parking the car.'

He laughed. 'My number one'll give it back to you. The old bastard owes it to me.' He struck his cane against the shoe of his shorter leg. It dangled about a hand's breadth over the ground.

I pulled out my wallet and gave his a hundred dollar coin. He grunted his satisfaction and put it in his pocket. Then he bent his head and looked at me. 'I've seen you somewhere before, mister,' he said, and pursed his lips in thought. 'Not so long ago, either.' He patted the tender scar tissue on his temple carefully with the tips of his fingers. 'I remember,' he said, and slapped me good-naturedly on the shoulder. 'It was in a dream. A sudden attack or something similar on a bridge. I remember a rail. An ambulance was there. Someone held a submachine gun pointed towards me. And you were running back and forth screaming, "Why did you shoot him?"' He nodded. The sunken eye gleamed a watery blue.

'That was in Damascus.'

'Strange, isn't it. I've never been there.'

'But your number one, as you call him, was there.'

He shrugged his shoulders and, lost in thought, contemplated the silver skull on his cane. Then, he took the mushy cigar stump from his lips and threw it away carelessly. He put his weight on his shortened leg as if he

were stepping down and then, with a flowing movement, changed to his good leg. A skilful circling of his
hips corrected the sideways drift, a direct result of his
distorted leg. His movements were exact and controlled
like an assembly robot's and yet his lameness had
something deeply touching and human about it.

'Do you see him often?' he asked.

'Not anymore, thank God. You know, he lost his job.'

'Impossible!'

'He made a terrible mistake in Damascus. He bungled
up an important mission he was on for the Pentagon.'

He struck his shoe with his cane and his voice boomed
with laughter. 'And they say copies are stupider than
their originals, because up here,' he pointed to his
ravaged forehead, 'the screws are a bit loose. But in our
case, it seems to be the other way around.' He shook his
head with laughter. 'He deserved it, the old bastard!' He
swung himself around and limped towards the gatekeeper's hut. At the door, he turned and raised his
cane. 'Many thanks for the hundred dollars, mister.'

I crossed through the park to the main building.
There were a lot of wheelchairs, but not many nurses.
Everywhere I looked, decrepit invalids were apathetic-
ally waiting for death. Compared to them, Andrew
seemed full of life. I pushed him in his wheelchair over
the asphalt paths through the park.

'You know, Roughtrade wasn't the mad scientist
some thought him to be. He was only . . . He was
unbelievably thorough. But . . . ' Andrew glanced up at
me over his shoulder, 'a genius is expected to be like
that, isn't he?'

I didn't answer. We were both silent for a time. The
chafing and grating of the wheels on the path was all
that could be heard.

'They're going to try and sew a pair of lower legs on
me next month. I accepted on the one condition that they

217

choose a long pair. I always wanted to be a bit taller.' If this was supposed to be a joke, it didn't make me laugh. 'It was a real shock when I woke up here and my lower legs were gone. Thank God, I was still dazed from the whisky we'd drunk the evening before. Yesterday, in December, I was on the beach in Batticaloa and today, I'm here and it's mid-April. Do you remember the fisherman and the column of fire in the sky?'

'Sure, I remember.'

'That was half a year ago for you, but for me it's been only four weeks.'

'Do you remember a man with gold teeth whose face looked as if someone had taken an axe to it? We met him on the Sultan Ahmet flight.'

'Of course, I remember him well.'

'He sends you his greetings. I met him just before I left Damascus. He said you'd often crossed paths.'

'I don't know him personally, but that could only have been Naim Sanduk, Roughtrade's slave trader. By the way, I've had time to study my biography in detail.' He looked up at me smiling. 'Many thanks for your help, Pete. I now know what happened. My kind seems to be very much in demand. About a dozen copies in four months. On occasion, there must've been several copies of me in existence at the same time.'

'Whatever happened to the recordings of the other scientists – Torre, Pazzi, Wordsworth, Nealon, Donsdorf, Rodestrom?' And Nancy Tanner's recordings, I thought to myself.

'Ashkenside from the CIA thinks Roughtrade destroyed all those recordings as agreed, except for mine.'

'And his.'

'And his, of course.'

'What's happened to it?'

'A copy's been made. It's amazingly good. God knows how he managed to improve the recording again and again.'

'Will he be taken to court?'

'That won't be possible, Pete. The recording is almost fifteen years old. It was made in the research institute.'

'Very clever. He knows nothing. Nothing about the kidnapping – nothing about slave trading.'

'He really doesn't know anything!'

'And the price for his return to a decent life – the research documents – was fouled up by the CIA. He very skilfully engineered the whole thing. It looks like a put-up job to me.'

'It definitely was a put-up job. That's typical Roughtrade. He just didn't see any other way out of the vicious circle of money, power and violence he was in.'

'But to have to pay for it with his life?'

'There was no other way.'

'Roughtrade really died in Damascus then?'

'There's absolutely no doubt about that. The autopsy has proved that quite clearly.'

'Aside from the container in his car, he had three other containers he'd had delivered before his arrival at the Sheraton early in the morning. There was a recording of you in one of them and one of himself in the other. What was in the third container?'

'Someone, who was in Damascus at the time, told me all about that. His name was Jerry Shirley, one of Ashkenside's men. They were all keen on knowing, because they thought it contained the research documents. Know what they found? You'll never believe it – it's absolutely mad! The recording of a hundred and sixty tons of gold bars. The fortune he'd amassed during those years.'

'He could've set up ten laboratories to continue his research!'

'It must've been like the fairy tale.'

'Rumpelstiltskin, you mean?'

'Exactly! Only there, straw was sufficient to make gold. However, in order to produce a hundred and sixty tons of gold bars using the copying procedure, you need a hundred and sixty tons of atomic gold dust to charge the turbulence chamber.'

'And what happened to that fortune?'

'Should you ever meet Naim Sanduk again, ask him!'

'He's one person I don't want to meet again – especially in one of my nightmares.'

I looked down at Andrew's head. The skin on his bald head was sunburned and freckled and had started to peel. His frail hands rested on the padded armrests. Suddenly, a feeling of déja-vu overwhelmed me. I held my breath and closed my eyes, but it didn't help. I looked on passively while Andrew's skull burst open in a bloody eruption and splashed against my breast and chin. I looked down at myself in horror. There was blood everywhere, running down my chest and arms.

'What's the matter?' Andrew asked. He was looking up at me. My hands were shaking so violently I could hardly hold the wheelchair.

Nothing, I wanted to say, but could only croak. 'Nothing.'

He bit his lower lip and nodded. He then set the wheelchair in motion with a resolute movement.

'Nights are worst of all,' he said. 'I'm plagued with nightmares of torture, invalidism and death. I'm held prisoner in horrible places I've never seen before and beaten and mistreated by men I've never seen before.'

Pearls of sweat had formed on the top of his head in spite of the pleasant coolness of the shade.

'And sometimes,' he said, 'I dream of those in the lab. But I'm the one screaming out their sorrow and despair. Startled and uncomprehending faces surround me. It's terrifying!'

We wheeled by a bench where a tall, thin man was sitting. He was about forty years old. He was wearing a light grey suit with a waistcoat and an expensive Panama hat. Andrew stopped the wheelchair.

'Cecil,' he said.

The man turned his head and seemed to be listening. 'Yes?' he said.

'It's me, Andrew. Andrew Baldenham.'

'Yes, yes,' he smiled. 'It's such a pity.'

'Can you remember Peter Kirk?'

'It's such a pity.'

'Peter Kirk is here.'

'Yes, yes.' He took off his hat, laid it on his lap and nodded to me in a friendly manner. 'It's a pity.'

When we reached the gate, I handed Andrew the cassette.

'What's this?'

'A recording of our last evening together in Damascus.'

'Oh, splendid. The conversation of two morituri – recorded for posterity.'

'Your profession of the indivisibility and indestructibility of determinism.'

He laughed.

'You should incorporate providence and justice into your creed,' I suggested.

'I've never come across them in life, Pete.'

'I've seen them today. It must be hell to live like this.'

'I wouldn't be so sure if I were you!'

'Isn't it hell where Roughtrade now lives?'

Andrew shrugged his small shoulders. 'It's a resurrection of the flesh.'

'Yes, the flesh,' I said with a shudder.

He held my hand as if he didn't want to ever let it go.

'I'll visit you when I'm on my feet again,' he said. 'I mean it literally.'

'You're always welcome, Andrew. You know that.'

'Say hello to Ruth for me!'

'Gladly, you know how much she likes you.'

He smiled.

'I'm on my way to Houston to talk about another mission. We'll see.'

'Good luck then!'

'You too!'

McEnroe came out of the gatekeeper's hut and raised his cane with its shining skull in farewell. 'Thanks again, mister!' he called.

They waved to me for a long time – the frail figure in the wheelchair and the stout cripple with the burned temples. At the turn in the road, they vanished from my rearview mirror. I put my foot on the gas and fled the place. Nevertheless, the look in Roughtrade's eyes as he'd smiled up at me continued to haunt me.

His eyes had had that vacant stare, glazed and soulless, like the eyes of the dead.

BRIAN STABLEFORD

INVADERS FROM THE CENTRE

Asgard was not an easy world to leave behind.

Not that Mike Rousseau wanted to get away from it forever — he just wanted to take a vacation back in the home system. But things didn't turn out the way he planned, and he was back again much sooner than he anticipated.

To make things worse, he'd been drafted again, and the job he'd been drafted to do was even dirtier than the last one, and every bit as dangerous. He still had his old enemies, but now he had new ones — billions of them. And his friends hadn't improved at all.

Of course there were compensations — another chance to get close to the ultimate mystery of what lay at the centre of Asgard. But it seemed that the inhabitants of the lower levels were no longer content to wait quietly until they were discovered. *They* had discovered the universe . . . and were trying to decide what to do about it . . .

Post·A·Book

A Royal Mail service in association with the Book Marketing Council & The Booksellers Association.
Post-A-Book is a Post Office trademark.

MORE SCIENCE FICTION TITLES AVAILABLE FROM NEW ENGLISH LIBRARY PAPERBACKS

		BRIAN STABLEFORD	
☐	50103 5	Invaders From the Centre	£2.99
☐	50612 6	Journey to the Centre	£2.99
		C J CHERRYH	
☐	50086 1	Cyteen	£4.99
		JACK VANCE	
☐	49733 X	Araminta Station	£3.50
☐	50256 2	The Augmented Agent	£3.50
☐	50257 0	The Dark Side of the Moon	£3.50
☐	50258 9	The Languages of Pao	£1.99

All these books are available at your local bookshop or newsagent, or can be ordered direct from the publisher. Just tick the titles you want and fill in the form below.

Prices and availability subject to change without notice.

HODDER AND STOUGHTON PAPERBACKS, P. O. Box 11, Falmouth, Cornwall.

Please send cheque or postal order, and allow the following for postage and packing:

U.K. – 80p for one book, plus 20p for each additional book ordered up to £2.00 maxium.

B.F.P.O. – 80p for the first book, plus 20p for each additional book.

OVERSEAS INCLUDING EIRE – £1.50 for the first book, plus £1.00 for the second book, and 30p for each additional book ordered.

Name ....

Address ....

....